Fire & Water

Brett shuddered. "You're saying someone tried to dispose of a body a bit at a time. He removed the hands and feet with a hacksaw, then found himself in a bath of blood. On top of that, he couldn't destroy even those small bits in the fireplace. He gave up. Took the rest of the body away – to get rid of it somewhere else – and then splashed petrol in the middle of the room. He lit it to destroy the whole bungalow in an attempt to hide what he did here."

The pathologist nodded. "If I were you, I'd look for someone with a strong stomach. Start with the local butcher." He held up another scorched finger bone and commented drily, "I hope you're not relying on fingerprints to identify the victim."

Have you read?

Look out for:

POINT CRiME

LAWLESS & TILLEY

Fire & Water

MALCOLM ROSE

SCHOLASTIC

Scholastic Children's Books
Commonwealth House, 1–19 New Oxford Street,
London WC1A 1NU, UK
a division of Scholastic Ltd
London ~ New York ~ Toronto ~ Sydney ~ Auckland
Mexico City ~ New Delhi ~ Hong Kong

First published in the UK by Scholastic Ltd, 1998

ISBN 0 590 11333 X

Typeset by TW Typesetting, Midsomer Norton, Somerset
Printed by Cox & Wyman Ltd, Reading, Berks.

10 9 8 7 6 5 4 3 2 1

For Deborah, Caroline and Julia
because I promised at CHEM999
Residential School, 1997

The setting of this novel – Oughtibridge, near Sheffield – is real, but the characters who populate the story are not based on the real people of Oughtibridge.

The pathologist's gloved hand reached down into the dark hole of the grate and foraged for a few seconds. Like a magician, he plucked out a small trophy, held it up and examined it closely. It was like a short burnt twig, as black as the graphite in a pencil, with a bulge at both ends. "That's the fourteenth," he pronounced grimly. "Another charred bone. The last one was a metatarsal from a human foot; this one's from a finger. A middle phalanx, I'd say. Before the place went up in flames, someone tried to incinerate a body in here – or at least the hands and feet." He popped the blackened stub into a clear evidence bag and labelled it.

He was lying across the remains of the floor, a couple of centimetres deep in wet debris and rubble. The arm of his white coat was filthy where he had delved into the void of the fireplace. Near his feet in the centre of what had been a living room, an area of the floor had been burnt away entirely, exposing cracked and charred joists. This was the place where the fire had been most fierce. And it had been very fierce. The lonely rural bungalow was little more than an empty shell with smoke-blackened walls. Water from the fire crew's high-pressure hoses had pushed the few damaged contents against the back wall. The acrid stench – an inevitable result of fire followed by water – was overpowering and disgusting. As soon as the cottage had been damped down and made structurally safe, a routine investigation had begun. Ironically, the bungalow stood beside Burnt Hill Lane, in an isolated dip just along from Oughtibridge Cemetery.

"So, where's the rest of the body?" Detective Inspector Brett Lawless called from the doorway.

"No idea, but it's not here. This is just a hands and feet job."

Brett's eyebrows rose. "Not someone getting caught in a fire accidentally, then. And not suicide."

"Obviously not. There's a good number of heat-cracked finger and foot bones among the ash in the grate. Nothing else. No torso, no head."

Brett suggested, "Maybe the person's alive and, no doubt, not very well in hospital somewhere. Minus hands and feet."

"Your colleagues who got here first checked with hospitals. No joy. Like it or not, you've got a murder, not GBH. My last shirt's on it."

From the gravel path, the chief fire officer eyed Brett suspiciously. He coughed loudly to make sure that Brett knew that he was still watching him like a vigilant teacher keeping an eye on a troublemaker. The firefighter had come across Brett three days previously at the site of a collapsed embankment in the centre of Sheffield. Despite the chief's instructions, Brett had entered the danger zone rashly and could have got himself killed. This time, the fire officer was determined that Brett would heed his warnings and stay at the edge of the room where the flooring was still secure. The damaged floorboards near the seat of the blaze would definitely not take the load of more than one person.

Brett had promised to behave himself. He had encroached on the smashed embankment only because there was a chance that there was still life inside: a young kidnap victim. It was obvious that this gutted bungalow could house only the dead. There was no need for recklessness. Unfortunately, there was no one to rush in and rescue. The fire had already done its grisly work.

Brett pointed to the hole in the middle of the room and asked, "Nothing down there?"

The scientist rolled over to see what Brett was talking about. The front of his coat was black through contact with the wooden flooring that had been degraded to brittle, blistered charcoal. "No. No body bits anyway."

"What caused it? A spark from the fireplace?"

"I'm a pathologist," he replied, "not a fire specialist. But I'd say it was too far away. Besides, when the brigade's fire investigator arrived, apparently she smelled petrol. Forensic's taken samples for tests but an expert's nose is good enough for me. It was an indoor bonfire."

Brett turned, sighed and took a breath of fresher air. Arson made him think of an earlier case that he'd prefer to forget. A serial killer dubbed the Messenger had attempted to kill his parents by shackling them inside their bungalow, dousing it with petrol and setting fire to it.

The scientist turned back to his job and continued talking without looking up. "The fire in the hearth was a deliberate attempt to burn the evidence, that's for certain. But whoever stoked it up didn't realize how difficult it is to incinerate a body. Ask any undertaker. Cremation isn't easy. Six hundred degrees before the body goes into the oven and an hour and a half roasting. In here, someone couldn't generate a high enough temperature to reduce a body to ashes. Not even a bit at a time. My guess is they thought the hands and feet would be manageable in a small fireplace. Wrong. Maybe they gave up after all the fuss and bother. Didn't move on to the rest of the body. Maybe it got dumped somewhere else."

"Has anyone checked the garden? Any freshly turned earth? Any funny bumps where a body might've been buried?"

"Better than that. Someone's scanned it, looking for underground soil disturbances. Nothing. I heard they swept across the field outside as well. Drew another blank. But I know how come the hands and feet got detached from the rest."

"Oh?" Brett prompted.

"Forensics found a hacksaw, twisted by intense heat."

Brett grimaced. The case was becoming more repulsive by the minute. He glanced upwards where there was only the bright blue sky. The roof had disintegrated in the blaze. "Blood?" he queried.

"Not visible," the pathologist muttered, salvaging a seared metacarpal bone while he spoke. "But the underside of the joists gave a positive reaction. What's left of the carpet was positive for blood as well. All over. A lab test will confirm it's human, no doubt. I suspect the room was awash with it." He bagged the bone and added, "That's another reason for thinking it's murder. If the victim wasn't already dead, he or she wouldn't survive an amateur amputation like this. The shock – loss of blood – would be enough to do in anyone."

Brett shuddered. The image that the pathologist had summoned was like a scene from a horror film. "You're saying someone tried to dispose of a body a bit at a time. He removed the hands and feet with a hacksaw, then found himself in a bath of blood. On top of that, he couldn't destroy even those small bits in the fireplace. He gave up. Took the rest of the body away – to get rid of it somewhere else – and then splashed petrol in the middle of the room. He lit it to destroy the whole bungalow in an attempt to hide what he did here."

"That's about the size of it."

"That's…" Brett struggled to find the right word. "Revolting."

"If I were you, I'd look for someone with a strong stomach. Start with the local butcher." The pathologist held up another scorched finger bone and commented drily, "I hope you're not relying on fingerprints to identify the victim."

2

In the short driveway to the cottage, Detective Sergeant Clare Tilley was standing next to the only fire engine to remain at the incident, talking to the local cop who had been the first police officer on the scene. "Who alerted the fire service?" she asked him.

"A chap driving past in the early hours. Calum Laidlow. He had a mobile phone."

"I'll need his address," Clare said. "Why was he on the road at…?"

"Three-thirty. Going home from an all-night party, he said."

"Couldn't have been that good if he left before dawn," Clare murmured. "Anyway, did he see anything other than flames?"

"No. Just the cottage on fire."

"OK." Clare flexed the stiff fingers of her right hand. There was an unpleasant dull ache in her right arm, tracing the path of a long ugly gash from the wrist to the elbow. A bandage protected the stitches that zipped together the flaps of skin. She had been injured the day before at the conclusion of the Chapman kidnap case. The scar would be a lasting memento of her violent part in the investigation. "So," she continued, "the fire crew arrived, checked no one was inside, put the fire out, and made the place reasonably safe. Word of the blaze got to you. You came along, looked around, and after a while called the duty sergeant for scene-of-the-crime officers. Why? What made you suspicious? In this weather," Clare said, glancing resentfully at the cloudless sky, "the house would've been baked dry. Ripe for a discarded fag end or something. It wouldn't take much."

It was the last Friday afternoon of July and the summer was breaking all records. Lowest rainfall. Most sunshine hours. Clare's face was bright red – as red as her short hair – and her nose was peeling. She had caught the sun on Tuesday, before she'd had a chance to stock up with sun screen.

"Even before the fire, it was a derelict cottage. Deserted. Kids from the town came up here, treating it like a playground. Fooling around. They weren't much trouble, though. Less bother here than what they might get up to on the estate, so we didn't move them on a lot. The fire investigator got a whiff of petrol when she arrived. At first, I didn't worry too much. I put it down to the kids having fun – dangerous fun – with matches and petrol. But then I thought about it a bit more. Arson's heavier than the lads' normal mischief."

"And why would they burn down their own playground?" Really, Clare was asking herself but she said it aloud.

The officer nodded. "Quite. That's why I asked for SOCOs. They've been pottering about ever since the ruin was declared safe. When they detected blood and found charred bones, I requested a senior officer."

"I'm with you," Clare said. "And it looks like your intuition was right. Seems that someone tried an amateur cremation. Very amateur."

"I requested a check on hospital admissions as well. Burns and loss of limbs. It turned up nothing."

Clare nodded. "Thanks." Obviously, the officer had been thorough and taken the proper course of action. "You'll get me the names and addresses of all the kids you know who came here?"

"No problem."

Clare and the policeman shuffled to one side of the drive as a couple of forensic technicians inched past on hands and knees, their noses to the gravel. They were grumbling that they hadn't got a hope of detecting any impressions of car tyres. The fire engines had obliterated the evidence of any other vehicles. It was always so in cases of arson. The firefighters' job was to put out a fire, not to preserve clues. They'd trample all over the place, break into the building, wash away evidence with jets of water, disturb debris that might have held vital clues, remove evidence in an attempt to make the site safe for investigation. No other crime scenes were as messy as arson and explosions.

Clare asked, "Do you know who owned the bungalow?"

"Sorry," the policeman answered. "It's been empty for ... ages."

"Do you know if the place had power? Gas or electricity?"

"No, I wouldn't have thought so. It would've been cut off a long time ago."

"Anyone reported missing in the area?" Clare queried.

"Nothing's come in, as far as I know. Not yet, anyway."

The forensic scientist supervising the scene-of-the-crime team approached and interrupted. "Ma'am?"

Clare winced. "Sergeant Tilley's the name. Clare."

"Sorry, ma'am ... I mean, Sergeant..." The young man called Neville shook his head at his own clumsiness and embarrassment. He looked up at her attractive face and muttered, "We've got a lot of stuff from the grounds. Like this." He held up a transparent evidence bag containing a small red penknife. "Not much from the cottage, though. Want an update?"

"Please," she replied. She pointed at the imposing outline of Brett standing in the black hole that used to be the cottage's doorway. Flinching at the pain in her arm, she said, "Go and ask him to join us, will you? The boss – and forensic guru. He'll want to be in on this. And," she added kindly, "he's not into formalities. His name's Inspector Lawless, not sir."

Neville said, "Thanks, I'll remember that," and walked towards Brett.

Brett held up the bag and examined the penknife. "Kids' stuff," he predicted.

Clare nodded in agreement but inwardly she shivered. She didn't like knives. She had been sensitive about them ever since she had seen her dad being attacked with one when she was thirteen. This one was harmless enough but she was concerned that its young owner might progress to more dangerous blades.

Knowing his partner's hatred of knives, Brett glanced at her before adding, "Not the sort of thing that's been used on the body, such as it is. But," he said to the forensic scientist, "get it checked for blood anyway – and prints, of course."

Eager to prove the team's diligence and value, Neville began to list their finds. "Outside, we got shoe impressions – lots of trainers – and tyre tracks from mountain bikes. Fibres, fragments of clothing, a pop music cassette – broken, pages from a girlie magazine, a pound coin. A small bit of plasterboard by the front door. Wet and charred paper, almost certainly wallpaper blasted out of the house by the fire crew's water jets. A half-eaten kebab, empty can of Lilt, cigarette packets and—"

Brett stopped the torrent by putting up his hand like an authoritative traffic cop on the high street. "OK, OK. First, tell me, have you got any real clinchers? Like, if there were any windows left, they must have blown out. Any fingerprints on the bits of glass?"

"We've separated the clean glass – smashed before the fire – from the smoke-stained stuff. No sign of prints on the bits that came out in the fire."

"What about inside? That's where the action was."

"There wasn't much inside. And most of it was ruined by fire or water."

"Any shoe impressions?" Brett enquired.

Even though it was Brett who was asking the questions, Neville kept looking at Clare. "Too badly trampled by the fire crew," he reported.

"Shoes and socks? I doubt if anyone would hack off the feet with the socks still on."

"No sign of socks. Probably ash by now," Neville proposed. "But, yes, we got shoes. Sort of. Mostly burnt, the rest melted. Cheap plastic. We won't even be able to tell you the colour or size."

"Man's or woman's?"

Neville shrugged. "One bit of melted shoe looks like any other."

"A lighter or remains of a box of matches?"

The forensic scientist shook his head. "We looked for them – but nothing."

"A watch or bracelet?"

Neville frowned. "I'm ... er ... not sure we've... Why?"

"Think about it," Brett said. "Someone's hacked through wrists here. What's going to fall off – apart from hands?"

Neville nodded. "I see what you mean. I'll go and make sure everything's been sifted for a watch or bracelet."

"Any rings? Particularly in the grate with the finger bones."

"I'll double check that as well but it might have to wait for the pathologist to finish."

It was difficult to raise a smile at the scene of such an awful crime. Clare suppressed hers before it reached her lips. But she enjoyed listening to Brett when he was in this mood. Inquisitive, logical, intelligent, a little impatient. Like the most determined cracker of cryptic crosswords. Obsessive even. He could not stop thinking about a puzzle until he'd solved it. Clare knew she had the most unusual partner in the business: someone with a real flair for facts. And by far the best-looking detective in the squad.

Neville noted, "We did find a bit of shrivelled cord inside. About a metre. Badly burnt as you'd expect."

"Can you say anything about the ends? How had they been cut?"

"We'll have to see in the labs but there might be too much fire damage to tell."

When Neville headed back to the wreckage to give extra orders to the scene-of-the-crime officers, Clare looked at her partner sympathetically and enquired, "Thinking about your mum and dad?"

Brett averted his gaze from the cottage. "You've got an uncanny knack for reading minds," he answered. He did not volunteer to reveal any of his private thoughts.

Clare knew that, during the Messenger case, Brett's quick thinking and bravery had allowed him to rescue his mum and dad but their home had been utterly destroyed.

Suddenly, Brett stared over Clare's shoulder and pointed across the sloping field at the back of the cottage. Clare spun round. A girl, probably about fifteen years of age, was standing with her right hand on her brow to keep the sun from her eyes. She was surveying the circus that attended the scene of any serious crime. When she noticed that Brett and Clare had spotted her, she turned and began to run back towards Oughtibridge.

Clare glanced at Brett and groaned. "I hope you're feeling fitter than me."

They both set off after the young woman.

It was Friday 25th July. A breathless afternoon above Oughtibridge, a small town packed into the valley of the River Don, on the north-western edge of Sheffield. Not a day for exertions. But Brett sprinted down the field, ahead of Clare whose injury hindered her movement. The pumping of her arms, the dash across the grass, brought a rush of blood to the gash. She could feel an uncomfortable pressure against the wound in her arm and a queasiness in her stomach. She did her best to ignore both, but she couldn't keep up with her partner.

In the distance, on the opposite side of the valley, the mottled green canopy of Wharncliffe Wood blanketed the hillside. Ahead of Clare, Brett vaulted over a rickety wooden gate, which collapsed under his weight. Clare jogged through the gap, jumping over the fallen slats. Two horses grazing in the next field looked up and eyed the three humans curiously but did not move. A frightened squirrel shot up a nearby tree for safety. The next obstacle was a low dry-stone wall. The girl, Brett and then Clare cleared it in a single leap. When Clare hit the ground on the other side, her arm was jolted and she winced with the pain. A small herd of cows ambled away from the crazy people encroaching on their peaceful pasture.

Watching Brett from behind, Clare noticed that his running was more ragged than normal. It had been a tough week for both of them: all work and little sleep while they laboured to trace a young girl who had been kidnapped. Now they had to chase an older girl – a fit teenager, this time. At least it was downhill and Brett was closing on her. The girl swerved on to a short and narrow path over a stream. The trail ended two metres above Wheel Lane. Stepping stones were set in the bank. Panting, the girl stumbled down them on to the tarmac of Wheel Lane and turned right towards the town. Brett made up a few seconds by leaping over the steps, landing directly in the lane. Clare was tiring and the lead weight that was her right arm throbbed, yet she was too tenacious and obstinate to give up the pursuit. Gingerly, she tackled the steps down to the tarmac. One after the other, the three of them sped along the track towards the sound of cars on Church Street. Clare heard Brett shouting after the girl, telling her to stop, but she didn't take any notice. She just kept on running.

The claustrophobic lane was lined with hedgerows, a stone wall and trees. On the left, a brook gurgled. Pigeons cooed from a loft on the right. Behind netting, chickens clucked in panic and geese hissed as the strange trio pounded past. At the main road, a tractor was plodding uphill with a procession of intolerant cars in its wake. It saved Brett and Clare from complete exhaustion. The girl, trying to cross into Poplar Road, came to an abrupt halt because of the queue of vehicles blocking her way. Before she made up her mind what to do, Brett caught her.

One of the cars stopped and the male driver leaned out of the window. Assertively, he shouted, "Leave her alone, pal!" He waved a portable phone and added, "I'm calling the police."

Coming to a halt at the kerb, Clare flashed her warrant card and replied breathlessly, "Thanks, but you're too late. We're already here."

"Oh. I see. All right." The driver pulled away and merged with the crawling cavalcade.

Joining her partner and the girl at the roadside, Clare looked sternly at both of them and gasped, "What did the doctor say yesterday? I'll be fine as long as I take it easy, get lots of rest." Her tone wasn't serious yet she held her swollen arm delicately with her left hand. A small stain had appeared on the bandage like red ink seeping across blotting paper.

"Are you OK?" Brett asked.

"I'll live," Clare replied.

Turning to the girl, Brett smiled and, in an attempt to relax her, joked, "Now look what you've done – aggravated a police officer."

It didn't work. The young woman did not react. She just stared defiantly at Brett.

"Who are you?" he asked. "What's your name?"

"What's it got to do with you?" she responded, her head held high. Her hair was jet black and short. She wore a T-shirt, black shorts, trainers and a serious expression.

Clare and Brett introduced themselves and then Clare took over. While Brett was good at squeezing information out of physical evidence, Clare was better than him at squeezing information out of people. "Now," she said, "we need to know your name – because, in our report, we've got to call you something."

The girl peered into Clare's face, assessing her, and then answered. "OK. I'm Debs. Deborah Pillinger."

"Good. That's better. You live near here?"

She pointed across Church Street and said tersely, "Poplar Close."

Clare noticed that Deborah's right hand bore a large plaster. She pointed to her own bandage and said, "Snap! What happened to *your* hand?"

Debs held her left hand over the injury. "It's nothing. Just caught it on some glass."

"Ditto," Clare replied. "Not nice." Then she

enquired, "What were you doing up there near the cottage, Debs?"

"It's a free country, isn't it?"

"Yes, but it doesn't mean you'll never be asked what you're doing."

"I can be curious, can't I?" Debs replied boldly with yet another question. "I wanted to know what all the fuss was about."

"Fuss?"

"Someone torched the cottage last night, didn't they? Word got around. Wanted to see what it looked like."

"That's fair enough. Do you know who did it, Debs? Who torched it? Has word got around about *that* yet?"

Deborah shook her head. Even if she knew, she wasn't going to say any more.

"Not even a rumour?" Clare checked.

"No."

Brett butted into the conversation. "You haven't done anything wrong. Innocent curiosity. I can understand that. So why did you run away, Deborah?"

"I'm a juvenile," she said defiantly. "Don't you need an adult around before you're allowed to question me?"

"A parent or social worker – if we make this official by taking you to the station," Brett admitted. "Is that what you want? A trip to the police station?"

Debs sighed and frowned. "No, I suppose not."

"Better tell us why you ran away, then."

"Because it was obvious you was cops. I don't speak to cops."

Clare asked, "Did *you* ever go to the cottage?"

"Only the lads go up there," she stated a little too quickly. She shuffled uneasily.

Aware that Debs had just lied, Clare looked into her face and said, "Do you know if some lads were up there last night?"

"No."

To Clare, it sounded like the truth this time. "Were *you* up there last night, Debs?"

Screwing up her face into a scowl, Debs snarled, "Do I look like a lad?"

They let her go, after warning her that they might need to speak to her again, and then they retraced their steps. While they trudged back up to Burnt Hill Lane, Clare reasoned, "Quite a few of Neville's finds smacked of kids. You know – bikes, trainers, a cassette. And a girlie magazine suggests boys."

"Yeah. Maybe they rode around a bit, played some music, broke a few windows, smoked a few fags, but I don't think what I saw was the work of kids," Brett declared.

"I wouldn't be so sure," Clare retorted. "Arson's more or less a teenage epidemic and gang warfare's on the rise these days. I know the local cop reckoned the gang he knew wasn't into arson, never mind murder. But what if a tougher, more malicious breed started to muscle in on the cottage? Maybe they got hold of a member of the first gang. Maybe a bit of aggro turned nasty. Maybe they didn't mean it to, but it did. Then they got scared and tried to cover up. That's when they tried to burn the evidence."

Brett preferred theories that were based firmly on facts rather than on instinct – even though his partner's instinct had been proved to be reliable. He nodded and said, "All right. It's a theory, I'll grant you that. But until we've got some evidence, it's just a story. Just a load of maybes."

"A plausible load of maybes," Clare stressed.

The mountainous Detective Chief Superintendent John Macfarlane sat behind his desk and lectured them. "Arson comes in three flavours. One: pyromania. Difficult to catch pyromaniacs because you don't know where they're going to strike. But they do have weaknesses – like reporting their own fires, often hanging around to watch their handiwork and doing it compulsively over and over again. Serious attention- and excitement-seekers. Two: grudges and revenge. Neighbours at war with each other, armed with petrol-soaked rags to shove through each other's letter boxes. And pupils with a grudge torching their school. That sort of thing. Three: evidence evasion. Fire used to cover up something else. That's what you've got. Usually it's insurance fraud. Not very profitable with a dilapidated cottage, though. Yours is something else. A murder, presumably. Where are you going to start?"

"Identity of the victim," Brett began.

Immediately, Big John interrupted. "You haven't even got teeth to compare with dental records. How do you identify someone through ash and a few lumps of cinder?"

The telephone rang and for a while the Chief Superintendent listened to the caller in exasperated silence. Then he exploded. "Not guilty! And I'm a supermodel! We spend all that time and energy getting these people and then juries … I'm amazed. Not even a majority guilty verdict!" He shook his head. "It's just like the last one. You know, in these complicated fraud cases, either the jury doesn't understand or someone gets to them. There's enough money sloshing around in fraud to buy off a few members of the jury." For a minute, Big John concentrated on the reply. Then he said, "Really? Well, get the Chief Constable's authorization, then look into it. If sizeable amounts of money have gone into jury members' bank accounts – if they've been nobbled – someone leaked their names and addresses to the bad guys. And Luke Kellaway would have that information. If he's earning on the side, I want him caught. I don't like bad apples ruining our efforts to put crooks away. Not good for my officers' morale." Big John put the phone down and growled, "Looks like we've got a seriously leaky police liaison officer at Crown Court, selling jury details to wealthy defendants in fraud cases. They bribe a few members of the jury to find them innocent." He cursed aloud and then muttered, "There's always someone out to make an easy, and corrupt, buck. Anyway, where were we? Ah, yes. Identification of your rather lean victim."

"There are some things we can do," Brett claimed. "Look for any jewellery. And the rest of the body. Door-to-door in Oughtibridge and Worrall to ask if someone didn't come home on Thursday night or this morning. We'll check people who've just gone on the missing persons' index as well. Then there's the chap who reported the fire. We want to speak to him. And we need to trace the owner of the cottage – if there is one – and interview the kids who played there."

"Don't forget you've got the site where the body – some of it – was disposed but you may not have the murder site yet."

"The door-to-door officers need to keep their eyes open and look into any likely spots."

"Sounds heavy on resource," John grumbled, "but I'll do what I can."

"You'll note we need someone who's good at sifting information and digging around in data." Brett prompted tentatively, "What about Louise Jenson?"

John let out a long sigh. After a few seconds of fiddling aimlessly with a biro, he delivered his brief verdict. "No."

Louise was a new recruit. She had been given an attachment to Brett's team on the Chapman case, but yesterday afternoon her blunder in the field turned a simple operation into a violent battle. Even so, Brett rated Louise highly and her research had been excellent. In her defence, Brett ventured, "You once said to me that we all learn this trade by doing it, making mistakes, learning from them, building up experience."

"True. But we don't learn by being let off our mistakes. She'll be out pounding the streets, controlling football crowds, attending domestic disputes and burglaries. If she's as good as you say, she'll bounce back the better for it." John leaned forward and announced, "You've got Liz Payn instead."

Both Clare and Brett smiled. Louise was good but Liz was the best.

"And Brett?" John called as they were leaving. "I don't need a lesson on staff management."

"Sorry, sir."

The driver's taped voice sounded remarkably relaxed and unconcerned.

Most people making a 999 call to report a genuine crime were nervous or shocked. They talked too quickly or too slowly, unable to explain clearly what had happened. Sometimes they were struck dumb. The calls varied from illogical to garbled.

Listening carefully to the recording of Calum Laidlow's emergency call, Clare observed, "Unruffled, isn't he? Mildly amused, even. Perhaps he's drunk. He'd been to a party."

"Perhaps," Brett said. "But is he surprised?" Brett was concerned that the early-morning driver might be trying to divert suspicion from himself by reporting his own crime.

Clare rewound the tape and listened again. "Cool

under fire," she answered, "but I reckon he's surprised, yes. Why don't you get the behavioural people – the phonetic experts – to have a listen and decide if he's reporting what he's just done? Or do you regard that as mumbo jumbo?"

"Not far off. But they might as well have a listen while we go and speak to him. That'll give us a better idea. Besides, we need to check for ourselves if he saw anything useful."

Outside in the corridor, they stopped by the drinks machine to get a cup of a liquid that approximated to coffee. While Brett ran through all of the jobs that were about to ruin their weekend, Clare stared distractedly into an interview room where a man in jeans and black T-shirt was sitting and looking pleased with himself. He was leaning back in his chair with his hands behind his head. He was about thirty with short hair, a stubbly chin and a small scar on the right side of his forehead.

Detective Sergeant Greg Lenton emerged from the room, shaking his head in annoyance. "The old story. Guilty as hell but I can't nail him. I'm going to have to release him so he can go and assault someone else."

"Who is he?" Clare asked.

"Adrian Telfer. A real charmer," Greg muttered resentfully. He headed for the custody sergeant to give the order for the man's release.

"Come on," Brett said to Clare. "Let's go and brief the team."

"OK," she replied. "But … just a minute."

To Brett's surprise, Clare stormed into the interview room. She reached across the table, grabbed a fistful of Telfer's T-shirt in her left hand and yanked him out of his seat. The suspect's chair fell backwards and clattered on to the floor as Clare's natural strength lifted him right off his feet. The edge of the table bit into his belly. Clare waved her right fist in front of him threateningly and snarled directly into his face, "Do you like music, then?"

"You what?" he mumbled. His expression revealed fear and astonishment. "You can't do this! Get your hands off me!"

"Like listening to it on a Walkman, do you, Telfer? Yes? I'm going to make you remember me! And remember my dad."

Aware that she could fell him with a single ferocious blow, Brett dashed into the interview room, shouting, "No, Clare!" He was followed by Bob Baird, the custody sergeant.

As the two men dragged her away from Telfer, she barked, "You're the one who knifed my dad and ran off with his bag. You nearly killed him for a twenty-quid Walkman!"

Recovering from the shock of her outburst, Adrian Telfer smoothed out his shirt with his hands and then laughed. "You've cracked, you have. I've never seen you before. I never nicked a Walkman."

Brett and Bob wrestled Clare away before she got into deeper trouble. Brett kicked the door shut with his foot and manhandled her into the corridor and out of sight of the interview room.

He held her by the shoulders until she had calmed down and said, "Clare, your dad was mugged twelve years ago! It could've been anyone—"

Angrily, she interrupted and shrugged him off. "Some faces you don't forget," she hissed as she turned and walked away.

Brett looked at Bob Baird and sighed. "No harm done, anyway."

"Are you saying I shouldn't report this ... incident?"

"Nothing really happened." In a hushed voice, Brett commented, "Isn't it up to Telfer to make a complaint?"

"Leave it with me," Bob replied. "To be honest," he grunted, "if it was up to me, I'd hold scum like him while she laid into him."

Brett understood Clare's desire for revenge. But if she had really decided to get her own back there and then, she could have done. Even with an injured arm, she could have floored him before Brett had got close. Something – a respect for the process of law – had stopped her. Brett was tired of hearing views like Bob's because the sergeant seemed to have no respect for the law. He was judgmental without the benefit of evidence and vindictive without the excuse of a vested interest.

"What is it about you, Brett?" Liz chirped. She

nodded towards Clare's bandaged arm and said, "Since you've been working with Clare, she always seems to come off worst. At the end of every case, she looks half dead. What are you doing to the poor girl? I don't know how she puts up with you. I hope you don't treat all your officers the same way."

Brett smiled. He'd never known Liz to be anything less than cheerful. "If *you* get hurt on this case, it'll probably be electrocution – by an overworked computer. That's all."

"I'm brilliant at other things, Brett. I'm not just a techno-genius."

"Point taken, Liz. I'll bear it in mind. But right now, I need to know who owns the Oughtibridge cottage and when they were last seen. I need a name on the victim. So, who's missing in the area?"

"But you don't know the victim's height, weight, sex, colour or age."

"True. That's why I need someone as good as you on the job."

Brett took Clare to one side and, looking at his watch, said quietly, "It's getting on. Why don't you call it a day? You must be knackered – and you are under doctor's orders to rest."

"You don't have to patronize me," Clare murmured. "You just have to say what's on your mind. You don't want me to attack Adrian Telfer again."

"I was thinking more about your arm," Brett replied, being slightly economical with the truth. "And I need you in good condition for tomorrow."

"You must be just as tired as me. It's been a long week. Your fish are probably getting lonely. They'll forget what you look like."

"All right," Brett conceded. "I could use an early night as well. Let's go and talk to Calum Laidlow, then knock off."

"It's a deal," said Clare. "It won't take long. People who light fires as a cry for attention or help call the fire brigade. Murderers who try to cover up what they've done don't."

Brett grinned at her. "Well, we both might be done in but at least *your* brain's still in working order."

Calum Laidlow was in his early twenties and he didn't believe in early nights. When Clare and Brett called at his house, he was getting ready to go out for the evening. He floated in an atmosphere of powerful after-shave. If they had struck a match, he would probably have gone up in flames.

"Where was this party on Thursday night?" Brett enquired.

"At my mate's. Over the hill in Bradfield. Near the reservoir."

Brett took down the details and then asked, "What time exactly did you leave it?"

"Exactly? It was … the exact moment they ran out of booze." He laughed at his own witticism. "Not really," he added. "I was driving. I left as soon as the girl I was after walked off with another bloke, damn him!"

"And what time was that?"

He shrugged. "How should I know? Some time after three, I suppose."

Brett would get one of his officers to check out Calum's story. If Laidlow did leave a party at just after three o'clock, he was out of the picture. He would not have had time to commit murder, get to work with a hacksaw, make a bodged job of destroying the body, and burn down the cottage before calling 999 at three-thirty.

Clare got the impression that Calum was too busy having a good time to embark on a killing. She remarked, "When you called about the fire, you didn't seem … perturbed."

"Why should I?" he retorted. "It was probably just kids. That place was derelict, you know. Not worth getting upset about." Repeating something that Brett had said earlier, he proclaimed, "No harm done."

He seemed genuinely to be unaware that great harm *had* been done to someone.

"Did you see anything – apart from the house on fire? Other cars? Any movement, any people around the cottage?" asked Clare.

Calum chuckled. "What do you want? Naked witches dancing round the pyre, chanting or screeching curses? If only! No, there was nothing." Once he had finished speaking to Clare his eyes lingered on her. He was getting into party mood already.

Clare turned away, saying, "Thank you. That'll be all."

Clare watched Brett feeding his tropical fish and observed, "Must be a pretty idyllic life for them."

"The fish? Why do you say that?" Brett took a drink.

"No predators," Clare said thoughtfully. "Watery heaven. No Telfers of this world." Sitting on her partner's sofa, holding a bottle of ice-cold beer, she glanced at Brett and said, "I blew it today. Blew my chances of promotion – again."

Immediately, Brett realized that she was talking about her confrontation with Adrian Telfer. "You'll be all right," he reassured her. "You didn't hurt him."

"But it was close. I could have clobbered him, Brett."

"Forget it. How's the Chief going to hear about it? Telfer won't file a charge. There's not a mark on him and he knows if he kicks up a fuss we might open up a twelve year-old case again."

Sarcastically, Clare said, "I can just see a jury believing my ID from all that time ago. 'And how old were you at the time, Sergeant Tilley?' Thirteen – a week off being fourteen. 'And how old was the assailant?' Late teens. 'Sergeant Tilley, how gullible do you think we are?' But, Brett, his image is etched on to my brain. Scar on his forehead. I can still see him holding the knife. I'm right."

"I believe you. And I bet Telfer's gullible enough to think we'll start investigating him again if he lodges a complaint."

"It doesn't matter," Clare said gloomily. "I know *you* won't say anything but…"

"What? You're saying Bob Baird will?"

"I doubt it. He's not one to be soft on crooks. But Greg'll get to hear about it."

"Greg?"

Clare explained, "Only one sergeant'll get promoted in the next round. Everyone in the squad thinks it's between me and Greg."

"He's … competitive, but he wouldn't…" Brett began.

Clare's expression brought him to an abrupt halt.

Mid-morning on Saturday. Clare wasn't out doing her shopping. She wasn't visiting her parents. She wasn't enjoying a swim or working out in the gym. She was listening to her partner in the incident room summarizing the meagre information for their team.

"This morning I received the pathologist's report," Brett announced. "A world record for brevity. The only thing he's got for us is size. The bones came from someone who'd reached adult size. Let's say, fourteen plus. That's it." He shrugged. "There's a body out there somewhere. We want it. And there must be people who know someone's missing. Keep up the door-to-door inquiries and follow up anyone over fourteen who seems to have disappeared off the face of the earth. And, while you're at it, don't forget to ask everyone if they've lost a hacksaw or had one stolen. Now, I spoke to Forensics and they haven't got a lot for us either. They've confirmed the presence of an accelerant – petrol – in the cottage. No surprise there. But no jewellery or watch, I'm afraid. And nothing worthy of being called a fingerprint on the bits of broken glass. There's a penknife, though. No trace of blood on it but it does have the dabs of a youngster called Joshua Redgrave. He's on our database for a couple of petty crimes. I'll go with Clare and have words with him today. We've got a charred piece of cord, too damaged to tell us anything. But since our victim probably didn't volunteer to be incinerated, it's possible he or she was tied up with it at some stage. Or it could just have been lying around the cottage for years. Anyway, it's worth chasing at hardware stores in the area. I'll do that as well. Liz'll sort out teams to look into recent additions to the missing persons' index. And Clare's got a list of quite a few boys known to hang out at the cottage. She'll organize who's going to check them out – and who's going to interview everyone at the Bradfield party with Calum Laidlow on Thursday night. Any suspicions or inconsistencies to be reported back to Clare. OK," he concluded, "let's get on with it."

The cigarette packets, drinks can, music cassette and magazine pages had also provided more fingerprints but, unlike Joshua Redgrave's, they did not match any entries in the national criminal fingerprint index. A careful examination of the shoe impressions suggested that there might have been a tussle outside the cottage and that one of the people involved wore a man's size ten shoes. The discovery was not very significant. Almost anywhere that teenage boys met bore the marks of scuffles. The tyre tracks, kebab, fibres, fragments of clothing and the coin had not yielded anything of interest. The small segment of plasterboard remained a mystery. The cottage was too old to have contained plasterboard and it wasn't the sort of material that wayward kids or firefighters might carry with them.

When Clare and Brett were leaving the station they walked past Greg. He gazed at Clare mischievously and wagged his finger exaggeratedly. "Tut, tut! Beating up my suspects – that's my job."

It was only a joke but it wasn't funny. Clare looked

at Brett and raised her eyebrows. "Told you," she muttered. Then, to change the mood, she squinted up at the relentlessly blue sky. "Another hot one." She slipped into the car and extracted a tube of sun screen. "I'll tell you one thing scientists got right: they may be drilling holes through the ozone layer but factor 25 saves my life."

Oughtibridge was only six miles out of Sheffield but it could have been on a different planet. It felt insular, enclosed by river and ridges. A place where everyone knew each other and strangers stood out like aliens, making them easy to shun. The original stone buildings of the town were lined up along the valley. Newer brick-built houses were stacked up the slope that led to Onesmoor. Poplar Road was two short established terraces that led to the more modern estate of Poplar Close. Walking along the closeted and inhospitable road, Clare and Brett noticed at least three people watching them suspiciously from behind twitching curtains. When the detectives arrived at Number 12, Joshua Redgrave's house, only his mother was in. Kath Redgrave was a rugged woman in her late thirties. She informed them sourly that her son was out at football practice and was due back in twenty minutes. While they waited Clare explained that, no, Joshua wasn't in any trouble this time but they needed to chat to him about the fire at the cottage.

Kath grimaced at Clare and said angrily, "It's

always the same round here. Anything happens and the fingers point at Josh. It's not fair on the lad. There's much worse youngsters. He won't have had anything to do with any fire. Sure, he's no angel but his heart's in the right place." She took a breath and continued in a slightly less aggressive tone. "Ever since his father left, Joshua's been…" She stopped, her gaze focusing on the window, and swore under her breath. "Just a minute!" She ran out of the living room, through the kitchen and out into the back garden where a big retriever was sniffing at her dustbin. She yelled, "Shoo! Go away. Pest!"

The dog looked at Kath, retreated a little, but did not scatter.

Determined, Kath picked up a spade and threatened the animal with it. Taking the hint, the retriever skulked away unwillingly.

When Kath returned to the poky living room, she complained, "Damn dog. Last week he had the entire contents of the bin all over the garden. You should do something about it," she said to the detectives. "Owners shouldn't be allowed to let their pets wander all over the place. Nuisance."

Not wanting to be distracted, Clare asked, "You were saying Joshua's been…"

"I don't know. A bit of a handful, some might say. But he's not … spiteful. Or stupid. He wouldn't start a fire." On hearing the front door open, she said, "Oh! Here he is. Early."

Joshua had cycled home on his mountain bike. His

shirt was damp with sweat. For a fifteen-year-old, he was a big lad. The first signs of stubble were showing on his chin and upper lip. It made him look rough. His face bore a striking similarity to his mother's.

To break the ice, Clare said, "Not the weather for football practice, is it?"

Joshua glared at Clare and, dropping into an old armchair with a can of drink that he'd taken from the fridge, mumbled, "We finished early. Too hot." He rolled the cold can across his forehead and then yanked on the ring-pull. The can opened with a hiss and a spit.

"Not exactly the right time of year."

Still hostile, Joshua said, "Manager doesn't want us to get rusty over summer."

Kath put in, "But that was the last session for a month, wasn't it, Josh? Till you start getting ready for next season."

He gulped down a large proportion of the drink, sighed and then answered curtly, "Yeah."

After Clare had explained that they'd come to ask him about the fire, Joshua snarled, "Why's everyone getting excited about a crap cottage getting burnt down?"

Unperturbed, Clare replied, "It's not the cottage we're worried about. It's what got burnt with it."

"What's that, then?"

Sensing that Clare was asking about more than arson, Kath was suddenly wary. She watched her son, shifting her penetrating gaze to Clare and then back again like a concerned spectator at a tennis match. Brett mirrored her movement as Clare took control of the interview.

"Do *you* know?" Clare enquired.

"If I knew, I wouldn't ask," Joshua snapped.

"Did you go up to the cottage with mates?"

"Not on Thursday night, I didn't."

"But you did at other times?"

"There's no law against it, is there?" he replied.

"Not really," Clare said. "What did you do up there? I bet it wasn't a study group doing holiday homework."

Joshua glowered, unimpressed by her banter. "Meet. Hang out."

Brett observed Joshua's yellowed right forefinger. While the teenager hung out in the dilapidated premises, he probably smoked.

Realizing that she was not going to get a more detailed response, Clare asked, "Did anyone stop up there overnight?"

"Not that I know about." He took another drink and then crushed the empty can in his right hand.

"Have you lost a penknife recently?"

"Yeah. Have you found it?"

"Up by the cottage – with your fingerprints. How about a cassette?"

"Don't bother with them," Joshua claimed.

Clare noticed that there wasn't any hi-fi equipment in the room, only an old television and video unit. "Do you know someone who's lost one?"

Joshua shrugged, not committing himself.

"Hacksaw?" Clare queried.

"You've got to be kidding!"

Brett put the same question to Joshua's mother. "Have you got a hacksaw in the house?"

Kath exhaled loudly and impatiently. "No idea. Maybe my ex-husband had one. He'll have taken it with him if he did. Like he took most other things."

Clare turned back to Joshua and said, "What about a rival gang? Was anyone trying to get in on the act at the cottage? Any aggro?"

"No."

"All right, Joshua," Clare said. "That's the lot for now. But I'd like to know where you were on Thursday night."

"Nowhere. I stayed in. Doing that homework you talked about," he said cynically.

"Is that right?" Brett asked his mother.

She nodded immediately and protectively. "The bit about staying in, yes. For the telly, not the homework," she said with a wry grin at her son. "Some blood-thirsty horror film."

Josh grunted.

On Langsett Road, the main thoroughfare running parallel to the shallow river, there was a cluster of old shops. Oughtibridge chippy, the village store, a newsagent, a hardware shop and a café. Just round the corner, there was a post office and two pubs. Before Clare and Brett went into the DIY store,

Brett's telephone squawked. It was Liz confirming that Calum Laidlow's schedule had checked out. Independently, two people had confirmed that he'd been at the party, chasing and annoying women, until at least three o'clock. One was worried that he'd had a bit too much to drink before he drove home. Brett thanked Liz and dismissed Calum Laidlow as a serious suspect.

It was a poky shop, the exact opposite of the luxurious out-of-town DIY supermarkets. Made of local stone, it smelled musty and old. There were just three cramped rows of goods, but it sold a wide range of hardware. Brett and Clare showed their IDs to the large man behind the counter. "And you are…?" Brett prompted.

"Jeff Pillinger," he stated coldly.

"Pillinger?" Clare queried. "As in Debs – of Poplar Close?"

Frowning, Jeff said, "Ah, it was you two who chased my daughter yesterday, then."

"Small world," Brett remarked.

"You won't get her now. She's out," Jeff told them.

"I want to talk to you, not her," Brett announced.

It should have been a small friendly shop – and almost certainly it was for the locals – but the owner did not take kindly to newcomers. "Oh?" he muttered.

"It's this." Brett produced the length of cord, coiled in a clear bag. "Can you identify it?"

Jeff moved a small stepladder out of the way and

took the bag. Holding it up to the light and grimacing, he peered at the cord inside. "God knows. It's been well and truly burnt."

"If you look closely, you'll see it's some sort of thin rope. Possibly that shiny orange stuff you get as guy ropes on tents and goal nets."

"Yes, I know what you mean." Jeff examined the sorry specimen again. "Could well be but ... it's a mess. Impossible to say for sure."

"Do you sell that type of cord?"

"Over there," Jeff replied, pointing down the middle row. "On a reel."

"Sold any this week?" Brett enquired.

Jeff shook his head. "Not one of my big sellers. Customers don't keep coming back for it. It lasts for ever – unless you set fire to it."

"OK, thanks," Brett said, taking back the evidence bag by its edge. He glanced round the shop and noticed a rack of saws on the left wall, including two different types of hacksaw. "How about saws?"

"That's a slightly better turn-round. I've sold a few, but don't ask me who to. I've no idea. Not to any of my regulars."

"Ah well, never mind," Brett concluded. "Before I go, though, you might be able to help me. I've got some cracked plasterboard at home. Needs replacing when I can get round to it. Do you sell it?" Scanning the shop, he said, "I can't see any."

"Plasterboard?" Jeff uttered, surprised that Brett was mixing police procedure and personal purchases.

"Does The King's Arms sell beer? Of course. But it takes up too much space here. It's out the back. What size do you want?"

Brett shrugged. "I didn't come out expecting… Anyway, once I've measured up, I might pop back. OK?"

Distrustfully, Jeff said, "Sure."

"Thanks for your help."

Before Brett and Clare could leave the shop, Jeff called, "My pleasure. Just don't speak to my daughter again without me being around."

While Clare's arm was still sore, Brett did the driving. Clare rested her left elbow on the lip of the open window as they headed back into Sheffield. The rush of air provided welcome relief from the stifling heat of the day. "Pillinger could have supplied quite a few of the finds," she pointed out.

"It wouldn't harm to take his prints off the bag with the cord, would it? Just in case they match those on the cassette, can of Lilt, or whatever."

"Not a legal way of doing it but useful, yes."

"If we get any matches, we can work out how to get his prints legally later," Brett decided.

"He wasn't a smoker," Clare mentioned. "No ash-tray and no smell. So I bet his dabs don't turn up on the fag packets."

"Yeah, but he does have another connection with the scene of the crime."

"Oh?" Clare said, running her fingers through her brick-red hair.

"His daughter, Deborah. She was taking an interest in it."

"You haven't come up with some fancy theory, have you?" Clare taunted.

Brett glanced at her and smiled. "Not on this amount of evidence, no. I was just … thinking."

Clare consulted the South Yorkshire map and commented, "Six churches in Oughtibridge, Worrall and thereabouts, according to this. It's Sunday tomorrow. Why don't you put a couple of officers into each congregation? They can ask around for anyone missing. See if any of the vicars think they've lost one of their flock. Even if they haven't, some of them have their fingers pretty much on the pulse of community life. In a close-knit community like this, you never know what they might come up with."

"Good idea. We'll do it. Chopping off hands and feet is a bit biblical, isn't it? We might come across one of those fire-and-brimstone vicars who advocates removing the hands of thieves."

"And the feet of … what?" Clare asked with a grin. "Footballers who commit fouls? Three red cards and they're off?"

"Wrong season," Brett declared. "But trespass happens all year round."

* * *

Back at headquarters, Brett assigned some officers to the next day's church duties and then briefed them. "It's particularly important you get a word with each vicar, priest or whatever. OK? We need an assessment of them all and their thoughts on any parishioners who might be missing or involved in extreme thuggery and arson. Anything from vague rumour to solid witness statements. Attending church – it's not a joke assignment. I want you to take this job seriously."

"Religiously," Clare chipped in.

"Exactly," Brett said. "The rest of you can pack the pubs as usual. Infiltrate. Ears open for any gossip. That way, we'll get a handle on the non-church-goers as well."

Then Brett organized a thorough search of the Oughtibridge area by the support group. He supplied grid references from the River Don, through the villages of Oughtibridge and Worrall to Coumes Wood and Onesmoor. To unravel the secrets of the dead, he had to find the remainder of the body. It was crucial to identifying the victim and identity was crucial to discovering the nature and motive of the crime. Without it, the team was blindfolded.

Afterwards, when Clare and Brett plonked themselves down next to Liz, she said, "You two look beat." She smiled and added impishly, "Burnt out."

"Very funny," Brett retorted. "Just tell me: whose cottage got burnt out? Any news?"

"Miss Emily Ashelford. Died five years ago at the

age of one hundred and fifty. Actually ninety-five. Never married. Sensible woman. No living relatives. No will. Didn't even leave it to a home for stray cats or something. It just withered away, like Miss Ashelford."

"Thanks, Liz," said Brett. He glanced at Clare and then continued, "Look, not much is going to happen for the rest of today and tomorrow, just leg-work. You're in charge, Liz. I'm ordering Clare – and me – to take a day off. We need it. Just call me if anything big happens. Like the body turns up. OK?"

"Yeah," Liz agreed with a grin. "You two go and relax. Enjoy yourselves and cool off. Have a swim and a few cold beers. I don't mind slaving through the unbearable heat all day Sunday."

"Come on," Brett said to Clare. "I'll treat you to a bite at my place – so you don't have to risk your stitches getting yourself a meal."

"I'm surprised you're not challenging me to a game of squash." She held out her bandaged right arm and added, "While you've got a chance of beating me."

"Huh! Fit or not, you wouldn't stand a chance."

While they sauntered away from the incident room, free for a while from the burden of the investigation, Clare said with a chuckle, "Really, you're inviting me to see your cracked plasterboard, aren't you? Maybe to help you fix it."

Both teasing and earnest, Brett replied, "I'm just feeling guilty about working you when you're injured. Overruling doctor's orders."

Clare smiled. "*That's* why you're being nice to me! Not so much resting my arm as resting your conscience." Of course, she didn't believe it. She was supposed to be good at judging character and she had long since concluded that her partner liked her company more than he'd admit. It was just over a year since he had watched a new girlfriend die tragically during his first major arrest. Clare suspected that his conscience still troubled him. She guessed that, deep down, he wanted to remain loyal to Zoe but he also wanted to forget and start afresh. And what would Clare's own attitude be? She knew the official line on affairs between colleagues. As a sin, it seemed to be ranked fifth – below corruption, incompetence, brutality and carelessness. But what of herself? Clare, not Detective Sergeant Tilley? Her own last serious relationship – with an artist – had long since bitten the dust, shot down by the heavy demands of police work. The romance had not survived the shift from the daily routine of eight hours' foot patrol, eight hours' free time, eight hours' sleep to the relentless and unpredictable schedule of the CID. She had done her best to work the disappointment out of her system. She tried not to grieve for it. But was she ready for a new relationship? At least Brett would understand the pressures of the job, and she always felt comfortable with him. But what sort of partner did she want Brett to be? A boyfriend or a colleague? The police force wouldn't allow him to be both. Right now, at the age of twenty-six, Clare wanted to secure her career. It wasn't easy for a woman to progress in the force and she did not want to jeopardize her chances by breaking an unwritten rule. Yet some sacrifices were very difficult to make. Like Brett. And some sacrifices were almost impossible to make. Like forgiving and forgetting Adrian Telfer.

On Monday morning Liz recounted Sunday's findings to Brett and Clare. "One string-'em-up vicar, eight boys who admitted going to the cottage occasionally, a dead cat splattered in the road. No missing persons but quite a few houses where no one answered. It's tricky because there's a lot away on holiday. No hacksaws or worshippers reported absent without leave." Liz glanced at her list and murmured, "What else? Ah, yes. A couple of arms."

Clare and Brett stared at her. "Arms?" they exclaimed together.

"Yeah. The King's Arms," she said with a smile. "And a few other pubs. No whispers in them, though. Strangely tight-lipped locals, even after they'd supped a few. The only thing we've got is what the landlord of The King's Arms *didn't* say. Name of Carl Greenacre. When our lot got there, they reckon he was talking about the fire with a couple of punters – blokes – but he shut up pretty quickly. It's one of those pubs that doesn't take to strangers. You might as well have sent the team in with CID tattooed across their foreheads."

"Pillinger's prints from the penknife bag?" Brett queried.

"Didn't match anything, I'm afraid."

"The gang of boys," Clare said. "Are they all telling consistent stories?"

"More or less. None of them talked about a heavier mob moving in. They all claimed bullying and arson didn't go on. Two mentioned playing music cassettes up in the cottage. One admitted glue-sniffing, the others denied it. Six said girls never went. Two of the boys, who were interviewed without their parents, said sometimes girls *did* join them. Deborah Pillinger and Chelsea Magnall were the only names they came up with."

"Not a lot, is it?" Brett groaned.

"Bet you wished you'd been here now," Liz replied. "You missed all the excitement."

Later, an e-mail message arriving at Liz's computer told them what they already knew. A phonetic expert had analyzed Calum Laidlow's taped voice and deduced that he was more likely to be frivolous than malicious.

It was late on Monday evening. A man dressed immaculately in a designer suit and carrying an expensive portable computer strolled across the notorious park where Clare's father had been assaulted twelve years before. The man was stylish but not imposing because he was short – perhaps five feet six – and thin. Not a prime physical specimen.

But his obvious wealth made him distinctive. Made him ripe for muggers. In the semi-darkness, he ambled across the grass and between the trees as if he didn't have a care in the world. Perhaps he did not know the area and realize that he was exposing himself to considerable danger.

It was more by good fortune than by good judgement that he crossed the short cut through the park without being attacked and robbed.

The investigation dawdled until Wednesday afternoon when word reached Liz that a male body, minus its hands and feet, had turned up in a reservoir at Bradfield. "Brett!" she shouted across the incident room. "At last. It's your lucky day. Not so lucky for your victim. He's surfaced – literally – in Damflask reservoir."

Brett strode towards the map on the wall. "Yeah, I know it. A mile and a half from the cottage, down steep and secluded lanes where a car brushes the hedges on both sides. Very convenient for transporting a body without being seen."

"From here," Liz announced, "you can best get to it up Penistone Road and out along Loxley Road."

Brett beckoned to Clare and, at the same time, responded, "I'm on my way."

"So's Tony Rudd," Liz informed him.

Brett smiled. "He would be." The chief pathologist was very predictable. Brett explained, "When a case gets bizarre, he always takes over from his colleagues. Loves intrigue."

"Want someone else to hold your hand, Brett?" Liz volunteered. "It won't be a pretty sight."

"We'll manage somehow. Besides, I need you here to assess anything more coming in, to communicate and coordinate." He headed for the door with Clare.

Ever helpful, Liz called out, "They say sucking extra-strong mints stops you throwing up and a hankie soaked in perfume stops you fainting."

Brett shouted back, "Thanks for the tip. We'll buy some on the way."

The large hollow in the moor was bordered by trees and, on the north side where the body had been dragged out of the water and on to the baked mud, by a stone wall. Occasional gaps in the wall allowed access to the water's edge for anglers. Further along, towards Bradfield, there were rowing and yachting clubs. It was one of the rowers who had spotted the body.

Several ducks swam across the water, leaving V-shaped wakes behind them. Bright yellow buoys were floating leisurely like decorative oil drums on the smooth surface of the water. Rowing boats and yachts with bare masts were tethered to them. The air above the whole area was thick with gnats. Kneeling by the body, Tony dispersed the haze of midges temporarily by wafting his arm in front of his face. He barely greeted Clare and Brett before he began, "One of my colleagues said the hands and feet were burnt in the early hours of last Friday. Body immersed for five and a half days. It fits. At this temperature, I'd expect a body of this mass to come to the surface in five days."

In death, the man still clung to his trousers but, if he had been wearing a shirt when he'd been killed, it had disintegrated or drifted away. The body was bloated and decomposing. His face and abdomen were particularly swollen with the gas that had accumulated as his body rotted. It was the buoyancy of this gas that had made him float to the surface. He appeared to be in his late thirties or early forties. Decay had discoloured his skin but he had clearly been white. This exposed skin was macerated – wrinkled and, in places, peeling away. Brett was beginning to regret not following Liz's advice.

"Not as interesting as I hoped," Tony Rudd proclaimed. "All pretty obvious. Cause of death: ligature strangulation." The orange cord was still tightly in place around the anonymous man's neck. "To be confirmed back in the mortuary, but I'd say it was hanging."

"A ritual execution," Brett murmured.

"Hands and feet hacked off very roughly. A saw." Tony pointed to the scratches on the bare bone with his gloved hand. Then he reached up to the victim's waist. "Same type of cord tied here," he noted. It was embedded in the soft, swollen flesh and attached to a sack. "Probably weighted down by rocks in the sack. Too many actually. The bag split, presumably when someone pushed the body overboard or maybe when it was sinking. Anyway, without ballast in the bag, putrefaction brought the body back up again right on schedule." As always, Tony hardly ever referred to his subjects personally. They never seemed to be a he or she. They were just characterless biological specimens.

"Pockets?" Brett queried.

"Nothing in them," Tony answered. "But…" He tucked his fingers under the grotesquely distorted chin and brought out a cheap gold-plated chain. "No ID but it's inscribed RW."

"RW," Brett repeated. It didn't mean anything to him. He phoned Liz and asked her to organize a forensic team. He wanted them to check all of the boats on the reservoir for traces of blood because he imagined that someone had rowed the body away from the water's edge before dropping it overboard. He also updated her. "Prioritize missing white males. Age thirty to fifty."

"Thirty to fifty?" she queried. "Not very precise. Presumably he's not in good shape. Hope you got those mints."

"Possible initials: RW," Brett told her, ignoring her jibe. "And there's something else you can get off the ground. There's yachting and rowing clubs here on Damflask Reservoir, Liz. Can you delve into them?

Cross-check members' names and addresses against everyone else we've got so far. I'd be interested in any matches. And see if any member reckons their boat was used, disturbed or hijacked on Thursday night, Friday morning."

Clare was still looking in sympathy at the sad remains of the victim. "Poor old RW. Not even a decent burial. Just fire and water."

The find at the reservoir transformed the investigation. Clare felt like a driver who had finally found the right gear and could accelerate away. Suddenly, there was a realistic chance of identifying the abused victim and the inquiry could take off. There was a heavy workload for the forensic scientists and for Liz. Much depended on Liz, her expertise with databases, and cross-referencing the information in them with the case details. On Wednesday night, when almost everyone else had deserted the incident room Liz was still there, straining her computer and herself to the limit. Her fingertips tingled, her eyes ached and her head throbbed.

Clare slapped her on the back and said, "Now you're the one who looks beat. Come on. Let's go and get a drink. And dinner if you fancy it."

Liz grinned. "Good idea."

"A girls' night out," Clare chuckled. "I haven't had one of those for ages."

Wickedly, Liz retorted, "You only go out with Brett these days."

"All very professional and proper, Liz."

"Professional. That's all? Are you sure? You're missing an opportunity there, gal. You could do worse than Brett. I have – several times." With real regret in her voice, she added, "Me, I've forgotten how to spell romance, never mind indulge in it."

"I meant, we live and work in such a male-dominated business, I can hardly remember socializing with just another woman – except in the gym changing rooms," Clare remarked.

Liz snorted, "Tell me about it ! Male-dominated – and white-dominated."

Clare slipped into the passenger's side of the car. "Do you still get that dreadful black bitch treatment? I thought it was over."

"Not so many messages, dirty pictures, racist and sexist comments these days," Liz replied. "It's more subtle now. Body language and the like."

Clare shook her head in disgust. "More snakes than ladders in this game."

Liz smiled wryly and declared, "I think *you've* got it sussed. All the blokes are scared of you. Scared you'll beat them up if they get on your wrong side. And they admire you for it. Me? Well, most of the white working-men's club accepts me now – probably because they can't do without my talent." She chuckled at the thought. She had overcome the worst insults with competence.

When they'd settled into Clare's local in Totley and taken a first long gulp of cold beer, Liz said,

"You came straight into the force from school, didn't you? Like me."

Clare nodded. "University or solving all the country's problems. Easy choice." Really, the knife attack on her father had influenced her decision. As a teenager she thought that she could help to make the world a safer, nicer place. She didn't realize then that she would be running hard just to stop crime dragging everyone backwards. Her father's mugging was also the reason why she had taken up several styles of karate.

"Me too," Liz replied. "Got out of school as soon as I could. I never got on at school. I was a pest. Head girl – of a sort. Head of a girl gang. I must have plagued the teachers but in those days you didn't think of them as real people who could be hurt, did you? Anyway, I carried on being a nuisance until one teacher parked me in front of a computer and said, 'Keep yourself out of trouble and don't break it.' Once I sussed it out, to me, the computer wasn't part of schoolwork – it was an *escape* from schoolwork. A magic box. Its monitor was a window on real life outside, beyond the school walls. It was great. I couldn't get enough of it. Like a fly to a flypaper."

Two men, leaning on the bar and talking in loud voices, kept leering at Liz and Clare. Liz shook her head pointedly in their direction and then ignored them.

Clare took another drink and said to Liz, "You're still eager to get out into the field sometime."

Liz nodded. "I can hardly remember what it looks like outdoors, but Brett handcuffs me to the computer."

"We'll have to see if we can do anything about that."

"The chief doesn't help. He came into the incident room today. Got me to do a bit of moonlighting. He wanted me to look at the verdicts in all trials where the juries were handled by Luke Kellaway."

"Ah," Clare said. "I know what that's all about."

"Once I saw the results, so did I. The number of not-guilty verdicts was way above average. I reckon the sergeant at Crown Court's been a bit careless with names and addresses of jurors."

"Yeah. That's what I heard," Clare replied. "Annoying. I'm just thinking how I'd feel if I'd been working round the clock for weeks to catch someone and Kellaway sold him the names of the jury so he could nobble them. I wouldn't exactly be delighted. Particularly if it was a really big case like a murder."

"I can imagine." Liz smiled at Clare. "You do love the big cases, the teamwork, don't you? You love the job."

"And barbecued red snapper," Clare said as her meal arrived.

Serious for once, Liz commented, "Don't mess it up – your career – by a revenge attack on some low-life, Clare. It's not worth it."

"Ah," Clare replied. "Does anyone not know about that?"

"I wouldn't have thought so."

"All right," Clare said. "I promise to stay on the right side of the law from now on." Keen to change the subject, she said, "I'll tell you what I liked at school: poetry, art, horror stories and football. Now I'm a Sheffield Wednesday supporter – a team that gives me a bit of poetry, sometimes artistry, usually horror."

"You should apply for the Football Intelligence Unit."

Clare laughed. "No chance. I'd watch the game instead of the crowd."

When they left the pub, they were approached by the two lewd and drunken men who had been boozing at the bar. In the car park, Clare and Liz refused their offer to go to a nightclub, but the flirtatious men persisted. One put his hand on Clare's shoulder and said, "What you done to your arm, love? I could make it better for you." He was not as tall as Clare and he smelled of lager. Not the most attractive proposition.

"How are you getting to this club?" she enquired.

Suddenly brightening, he answered, "You can come in my car, love. I'll drive."

"Sure you're going to drive?"

"Yeah," he answered eagerly.

Clare lifted his hand from her shoulder as if it were an irksome insect and then dropped it. She produced her warrant card and said with a sweet smile, "Not your lucky night, is it?"

On Thursday morning, the final day of July, RW's naked body was lying on a slab in the morgue, where Tony was working on it like a DIY enthusiast at a workbench. He looked up at Brett and said, "I got a forensic expert in before undoing the cords. You can sometimes tell whether a left- or right-hander tied a knot. In this case, though, no chance. But they've taken the pieces of cord, jeans, the sack and gold chain for tests." He lifted a bean-shaped kidney from the corpse and slapped it on to the balance to weigh it. While he continued the autopsy, he spoke to Brett and Clare. "Right. My domain. Cord tucked under the chin, rising at the back of the head. Fracture in the spine in the mid-cervical portion. A typical hanging – with a drop of at least one metre. No obvious wounds except for the strangulation and amputations, but discoloration would obscure any bruising. Facial distortion so I haven't got a photo suitable for general circulation. The dentist'll be in later to examine the jaws. Then you can confirm identity through dental records.

"Estimated height: five foot ten. Very short dark hair. Eye colour not reliable after immersion. Teeth suggest thirty-five to forty-five years old. Scar from appendix operation. Most of the blood remaining after the amputation is in the reservoir, feeding the fish. But I got some from deep thigh muscle. It's gone for grouping and DNA. Time of death: unreliable. But decay is consistent with five or six days' immersion. Now for the insides. Non-smoker, heavy drinker. Stomach contents: fish and chips consumed within three hours of death." He paused and, with a pathologist's typically sick sense of humour, said, "Not a very healthy meal." Drily, he continued, "X-rays show a repaired broken right arm. Linear bones show two hypoplastic lines, meaning two serious illnesses retarded growth at ages of about two and four. Nothing else yet. That's all the edited highlights for now."

"Any adhesive around the mouth, near the wrists or bottom of the trousers?"

"Not visible." Tony looked up for a moment and said, "You're thinking tape could have been used for gagging or tying wrists and legs."

"If I was being hanged, I'd create a racket and lash out unless something stopped me," Brett explained.

"If he'd been tied with cord, it'd probably still be attached to him."

Tony nodded. "But tape could have washed away. I'll do a microscopic examination for glue. You'll have to get Forensics to check the trousers."

"Thanks, Tony. You got more than I hoped for. We'll pin a name on him now." Brett asked Liz to circulate the dead man's description to all police forces, requested electron microscope and X-ray analysis of the bottom of the trousers, and then travelled back to Oughtibridge with Clare.

"Cod and chips and a veggie pie with chips, please."

It was lunchtime and, as usual, Clare and Brett were grabbing a meal on the move. The woman behind the counter had served her previous customer with a smile but it faded when she turned to Brett. While she shuffled chips into a bag for him he said to her, "I guess you don't get very busy on Thursday evenings."

The woman glanced at the man behind the fryers, almost certainly her husband, and then turned back towards Clare and Brett. "Thursday evening?"

"DI Lawless and DS Tilley," Brett replied, displaying his warrant card.

"What's this about, then?" she asked. She slapped a long, thin portion of fish across the bulging bag of chips. "Salt and vinegar?"

"No, thanks. As it is," Clare answered.

Brett asked, "Who came in and bought fish and

chips last Thursday evening?"

The woman turned away to get the second meal. Over her shoulder, she said, "It wasn't that busy, no, but I can't remember everyone. A few regulars – locals who always come in on Thursday – and a few people I didn't know."

Clare noted that she kept her face hidden from them as she answered. Her husband watched her while she was serving and speaking but Clare could not interpret his expression – other than the fact that he was apprehensive.

"Do you want these wrapped separately?" she asked.

"Please," Brett replied, leaning over the counter and taking a chip. Before putting it in his mouth, he said, "I don't suppose you've got security surveillance inside or out, have you?"

The woman snorted. "We're not made of money, you know. Besides, this is Oughtibridge, not Sheffield city centre."

"OK," Brett said. "But tell me, who were the ones you knew? It'd be helpful to know."

"Why's that?"

"I'm afraid we've recovered someone's body from near here. Someone who'd been eating fish and chips. We want to identify him – and hopefully rule out all of your customers. I'm sure you'd want to help us do that."

After taking a note of the names that she dictated, Clare asked, "And the ones you didn't know? Can you describe them – especially their ages."

The woman returned to the counter to wrap the meals. "Let's see… It's not easy to remember." She hesitated and then started to recall her Thursday customers. Some young lads wanting bags of chips, a couple of pensioners, a middle-aged mother with two or three noisy children. No one who resembled RW.

"OK, thanks," Clare said when the woman ran out of recollections.

"And thanks for these," Brett added, picking up the white bundles with their seeping grease stains.

"You're welcome," she responded in a tone that suggested the opposite.

Clare and Brett stood on the road bridge. While they leaned on the wall and ate lunch, the retriever that had plagued Kath Redgrave came up to them. Nose twitching, the dog put his paws on the top of the brickwork and joined them watching the river. He also kept his eye on their food.

They had already been in the café and listened to an equally vague, unhelpful and uncertain list of diners who might or might not have ordered fish and chips on Thursday. "Why does no one round here know anything?" Brett muttered in frustration. He held out a chip to the dog, who snaffled it so eagerly that he nearly nipped Brett's fingers.

"I get the impression that everyone round here knows something but they're not saying," Clare ventured. "Not to us foreigners, anyway."

"After this," Brett said, holding up the remains of

his unappetizing oily chips, "let's go and see Carl Greenacre in The King's Arms." He nodded towards the pub on their left, just into Church Street. "See if he's as reserved as all the others."

Clare devoured the last few of her chips and screwed up the paper.

Brett grimaced at the dregs of his own meal. "Good pie but the chips are a bit greasy." He was about to fold up the paper when the dog nudged him with an eager snout. With a smile, he said, "Keep that nose to yourself. You've had it in the bins." Brett studied the retriever's imploring expression, an undoubted Oscar-winner, and muttered, "Oh, all right. Not too greasy for you, eh?" He had hardly shovelled the chips on to the ground at the dog's feet before they had been wolfed by the hungry hound.

When they crossed the main road to reach The King's Arms, the dog followed them, strolling across the road as if he expected any cars to make way for him. He owned the centre of the village and he had right of way. When Clare and Brett walked into the pub, the retriever stopped at the door and growled ferociously until the door swung shut, excluding him.

Behind the old-style bar, Carl Greenacre was a short stout man with red cheeks like a clown. The top of his head was completely bald and highly polished. From the sides, level with his thick eyebrows, bushy black hair grew down, covering his ears. The effect resembled a giant marble egg protruding from a bird's nest. He looked the part of a genial host or a fool but Clare thought that, behind his easy smile, there was an unsettling hint of malice.

In the almost empty pub, with the dog's barking still audible, Brett asked Carl, "Do you have a male customer, white, about forty, who's a heavy drinker?"

"Sure. I've only got a few who aren't," he answered with an inane grin. "That's right, isn't it, Maureen?" he called to a woman who was wiping spilt drinks from the surface of the bar.

"How about one who hasn't been in since last Thursday?" Clare enquired.

Carl scratched his chin. "Last Thursday? That's narrowed it down quite a bit. I don't think so." He resumed the polishing of glasses until they were as reflective as his head.

"Initials of RW," Brett added.

Carl's hand inside the beer glass stopped momentarily. He was both puzzled and surprised. "RW," he mumbled to himself. He shook his head. "No, I don't think so." He shouted, "We don't know a chap, forties, with initials RW, do we, Maureen?"

The woman shook her head. "No."

"Sorry," the landlord said to Clare and Brett. He looked away and continued his work.

Outside again, on the gravel path that led to the garden and car park, Clare said, "There's your answer: he knows something but he's as tight-lipped as the rest. And a bit cranky, I reckon." She was getting annoyed with the conspiracy of silence that hung over the town like a persistent fog.

The retriever had moved on. He was scrounging from the café further along the row of shops.

Clare and Brett drove up Church Street, into Burnt Hill Lane and back to the sad cottage. Getting out, Brett surveyed the field around the blackened shell. "When he was hanged he dropped a metre or more, so how was it done?" Brett mused. "If it was here, I guess the cord would be tied round an exposed rafter. It'd be tricky – to say the least – for someone to hold him a metre off the ground and tie a cord round his neck. I reckon RW was pushed up on something quite high – some sort of platform that was kicked away to hang him. There wasn't anything in the cottage that would do the job, so it was wood and burnt completely to ash or it came out before the inferno."

Clare shielded her eyes from the sun. "Can't see anything out here that would do."

"So, if it survived the fire, it went away with our killer."

Clare deduced, "Must have had a biggish car or a van or something."

"Exactly," Brett murmured.

Before they left Oughtibridge, they checked out the regular customers who had called in at the chippy the previous Thursday night. The ones that they found were alive and kicking and the ones that they didn't were away on holiday. Descriptions forced out of surly neighbours eliminated the holiday-makers as candidates for the victim.

The initial optimism about identifying RW was receding. Back at the forensic unit, Clare and Brett heard Neville's verbal report. The sack had been identified as a light canvas bag, probably the sort used to store a tent. The maker's tag had been pulled off the material and it was mass-marketed, so an attempt to trace its source was unlikely to produce results. The cord was the stuff used for tent guy ropes and many other purposes – as sold in Pillinger's shop and a hundred other places. The victim's trousers were cheap and nasty jeans, to go with the poor quality shoes. His gold-plated chain was actually rather grubby. At a glance, it might have appeared chic but it was the sort of chain that was sold at plenty of dodgy market stalls throughout the country.

They left Neville to continue and complete the tests and headed back to the incident room. In a narrow corridor, they walked past Bob Baird. "Any news of the … incident with Telfer?" Brett whispered.

Bob glanced at Clare and smiled. "No problem," he replied. "Nothing's been said. Let's hope Greg gets something that sticks on him next time."

Clare nodded.

"It makes me mad," Bob continued with hardly a break for breathing, "seeing all those crooks like Telfer walking free from the cells. The crooks who slip off the evidence like it's a greasy pole. The corrupt ones we all know are guilty but with clever-clogs lawyers. I unlock the cells and have to let them go. You know who I had in here for twenty-four hours yesterday? Luke Kellaway – Sergeant at Crown Court. A sergeant! Drives a Jaguar, owns a posh place with a tennis court. All on a salary like mine. But he hasn't been selling jury lists – of course not!" he said, his tone dripping sarcasm. "You know, the SIO couldn't touch him. Top lawyer and non-stick evidence. All circumstantial. Soul-destroying. He walked away. And he's going to help others walk away from the courts by giving them what they need to nobble juries. It undermines everything we try to do. I hate it."

Brett was anxious to get on with his own case but he took time to sympathize. "It's … discouraging, for sure," he said. "But we've got to carry on. What else can we do? Frame them? Bending the evidence makes us as bad as them. Keep going and we'll get them one day."

"Thanks for the lesson," Bob grunted.

Hurrying away, Clare chuckled at her partner. "First lecturing Big John, now Bob. Ever thought of a job as a preacher?"

"Don't I chase enough devils already?" Brett joked. He burst in through the door of the incident room and cried, "Liz! Tell me you know who our victim is."

"You mean you want me to tell a fib?"

Brett groaned and cursed. "All right. Tell me

about the yachting and rowing folk instead."

"Drawn a blank so far. Most live in Sheffield, only a few in Oughtibridge. They're not people you've already interviewed. We haven't traced them all – quite a few on holiday. No one's reported their boat being disturbed but most haven't been to the club to check. I found one with initials RW but she doesn't match the rest of RW's description. Ruth Wallace."

"Anything else?"

"I'm going through every list I can get my hands on, like the telephone directory and electoral register. I'm finding a few RWs in the area. If they're male, about forty, I'm getting the team to phone or visit. So far, all in the land of the living. Oughtibridge or away on holiday – like sensible folk. At the moment, we're still working on Robert Watson and Richard Worth."

"Keep it up, Liz. Let me know as soon as you've got anything."

"First thing I'm going to get," she retorted, "is an extra-strong coffee." She got up, flexed her tired fingers, and ambled down the corridor to the drinks machine.

When Liz returned with a full polystyrene cup, somehow she looked less jaded, more optimistic. She put the coffee down beside the keypad and immediately contacted the National Identification Service and logged on to the Police National Computer. "Come on, come on," she muttered to herself. Suddenly she was on a high.

Clare put her left hand on Liz's shoulder and said,

"I don't know what they put in the coffee but I want some as well."

"I've just had an idea," Liz explained without looking up. "It's not the coffee but, if you go down to the machine, you might get the same idea."

Within half an hour, Liz sat back and beamed. Her screen was half-filled with the image of the dead man as he used to look before water and decay bloated him. The other half of the screen was crammed with information. He was a man who was very well-known to Thames Valley Police Force. "Brett! Clare!" Liz bellowed. "Come and get it! Come and tell me I'm brilliant."

Brett looked over one shoulder and Clare over the other. "Tom Grayson," they chimed in unison.

Clare studied the picture. "It certainly looks like him."

"Forty-two years old, single," Brett read. "But not RW."

Liz pointed to the bottom of the page of information. "Real name: Ray Woodman." Scrolling to the next page, she said, "You'll like this. Medical records. Chicken pox at two, mumps at five. Just what you wanted to match the autopsy. Appendix operation. Broken arm – probably the result of a battering by his dad who thought he could beat his boy out of being a sickly child. Regularly abused by his father, it seems. And at school, frequent reports of bruising – courtesy of the same monstrous father. Unhappy lad."

"Don't tell me he waited to middle age, committed suicide and someone tried to cover it up."

"I don't think so," Liz replied. "He found a different outlet for his frustrations. Earlier this year he was released from prison. Served six years of a nine-year sentence for child abuse."

Both Clare and Brett sighed. "His father made him the man he was, then," Clare said. "He was one of those victims of abuse who react by becoming abusers. He couldn't break the chain. Tragic."

"He was a newcomer to Oughtibridge," Liz told them. "Arrived a month ago. Presumably that's why you didn't get a whiff of him from door-to-door inquiries. He'd hardly settled in. His social workers probably suggested a change of location – where his neighbours wouldn't know his background. That way, he might stand a chance of leading a normal life, of integrating. Clean slate and all that. Even a new name: Tom Grayson. Not much of a fresh start, though, was it?"

"Certainly didn't last long."

Liz commented, "I've got his dental records here. I'll pass them on to make sure they match the odontologist's findings on the body."

"Thanks."

Curious, Clare asked, "How did you crack it, Liz?"

"It's a hi-tech police force now. Computers. Databases for almost anything. The information age."

"So…?" Clare prompted.

"I looked on the notice-board by the coffee machine. There's a description of abusers coming out of prison and settling on our patch."

"How many times have I walked past it in the last week?" Brett shook his head and smiled wryly. "Then I suppose you checked the offender register."

"Easy-peasy."

"OK," Brett murmured. "Let's see some progress. Who do we want to talk to? His social worker or supervisor. His victims, obviously, in case one caught up with him and got their own back. Motive: revenge."

"His family. His dad," Clare stated.

Brett grimaced. "Now there's a pleasant prospect. And I'll have to get someone from Thames Valley to break the news to them."

"I'll check local papers," Liz volunteered. "If the press got wind of an offender like him moving into the area, they'd probably run a crusade to drive him out again."

Brett nodded. "Good idea. But they shouldn't have been able to find out. Check who did know who Tom Grayson really was, Liz. Apart from ourselves."

"We ought to visit his neighbours," Clare said. Reading his address from the monitor, she noted, "An area we're familiar with: Poplar Road. We should take a peek inside his house as well."

"Yeah. And get the team out on the streets with copies of this photo, Liz. Ask around. Did he have a job? Where did he hang out? Who did he meet? Do they know his history? Has he been seen around school playgrounds? Ask the teachers, parents and kids. Anything."

Liz suggested, "I can check if he had a new circle of friends up here."

"Oh? How?"

"A new toy, courtesy of BT," she announced. "To charge its customers, BT keeps a record of every phone call made by every customer. We can request that information. Usually needs the approval of Assistant Chief Constable or above but BT isn't that fussy. A meagre detective inspector will do. I start by finding out who Grayson called. Then I use iTel or CaseCall: intelligence software that'll convert the information into a chart of names and addresses of people who are in regular contact over the phone. A circle of friends and family – no problem."

"It sounds underhand – a bit Big Brother – to me," Brett objected.

"I don't think Tom Grayson will mind," Liz retorted.

"I know," Brett said. "For his sake, let's do it, Liz."

With the cooperation of Thames Valley Police and Buckinghamshire Social Services, Clare and Brett talked gingerly to each of Woodman's three victims on Friday morning. Two of them were incapable of murdering anyone. They skulked aimlessly and stared at the ground nervously as if always expecting to be shouted at or hit, too devastated and damaged to be a danger to anyone else. And their angry, vengeful families had alibis for last Thursday. The third, an eighteen-year-old lad called Nathan Shaw, was different. He was clearly compensating for the wrongs done to him by becoming aggressive himself. He gnawed on chewing gum as if he were punishing it with his teeth. He also told Clare that Woodman was sending him threatening letters, colouring books and toys through the mail.

"Books? Toys?" Clare probed.

First, Nathan showed them a picture book coloured furiously and entirely in black and crimson. Then he produced a furry dolphin with a long nail sticking right through its soft head.

Clare grimaced at the perverse plaything. It took a warped mind to do such a thing. "I think we'd better take that, Nathan," she said, holding out her hand. "How do you know it came from Woodman?"

"I just know," he answered. "And there's the letters."

"Can I see one?" asked Clare.

Expertly, Nathan spat his used chewing gum into the waste bin and went out to fetch a letter.

As soon as Nathan was out of sight, Brett jumped out of his seat and delved into the bin. Wrapping the white ball of chewing gum in the waste paper to which it had stuck, Brett slipped it into his pocket. He was back in his seat before Nathan returned with an opened envelope and a fresh piece of chewing gum to pulverize mercilessly.

Clare and Brett leaned forward and examined the envelope together. The address had been printed by hand. "Posted a couple of weeks ago here in Milton Keynes," Brett observed.

Clare had not told Nathan that his tormentor was dead. She asked, "Nathan, do you know where he lives?"

"Sure. As far as I know he's over on Fishermead."

"In Milton Keynes?" Clare checked.

"Yeah." Nathan narrowed his eyes and added nastily, "I can almost smell him."

Clare ignored the peculiar remark but noted that he didn't seem to realize that the man who had wronged him had moved away, changed his name and died. "Have you had any more letters since this one?"

Nathan's jaw worked obsessively. "No. That's the latest."

Inside, there was a note hand-written in large capital letters. I'M OUT. BACK IN BUSINESS. R.I.P. The letters were ugly, angular and harsh.

Brett sighed in sympathy and murmured, "You shouldn't have to put up with this. Very unpleasant." He could not easily put his distaste into words. He could only pursue the truth. "For your sake, I'd like to prove who wrote it, Nathan. Did you keep any others?" he queried.

"Upstairs," Nathan stated. "Three more."

"With envelopes?"

"I threw them out."

"It'd be best if we took them away – and this one with its envelope," Brett said. "We might be able to find out where they came from." Brett was hoping that the forensic scientists would be able to get a DNA sample from the licked gum of the envelope or the back of the second-class stamp.

Nathan looked bemused but shrugged and muttered, "Anything if it'll stop the letters. I can do without them. The man's ... a monster."

Clare nodded supportively. "Let's change the subject," she said. "Do you get out much, Nathan?"

In surprise, Nathan frowned at her. "Course I do."

"Like where?"

"All over," he bragged.

"Have you been up north recently?"

"Not really," he replied evasively.

"Last week?"

"I meant, all over round here."

"You stayed around Milton Keynes with friends?" Clare said, as if she were indulging in sociable small talk, enquiring innocently into his private life.

"I've got lots of mates," Nathan claimed. "Out with them most nights. Tuesday, Thursday, the weekend."

In his sunken eyes, Clare read a different story. A loner with imaginary friends. But Clare did not wish to add to his anguish by testing his alibi for Thursday night. If she asked for the names of people he professed to be with on Thursday, he'd either invent them or crack up. She would pursue that line of inquiry only if they found any other evidence against him. "All right, Nathan," she said, terminating the interview. "I'm sorry we've had to put you through this. We'll let you know about this stuff you've been getting through the post. Thanks for your help."

"Put Woodman back inside," Nathan cried. "Where he belongs!"

Stranded in the desert of Milton Keynes, Clare and Brett took an early lunch – an Indian meal in the town centre – before interviewing Mr and Mrs Woodman. The detectives felt that they would need the sustenance.

"What was that with the chewing gum?" Clare queried, relishing a king prawn bhoona.

"With any luck, it'll give us a DNA sample from his saliva – trapped inside the gum," Brett replied. "If we get any DNA samples from the body or clothing that aren't Woodman's, they'll probably be the culprit's." Tapping his pocket where he had secreted the unauthorized specimen, he added, "We can match it with Nathan's – just in case he's lying and he did go up to Oughtibridge to get his revenge."

Clare waved her fork in the air. "Bet you the bill for the meal he's telling the truth. Doesn't even know Woodman's dead."

"The truth? Even when he boasted about his hectic social life, especially last Thursday?"

Clare admitted, "OK, that bit was a fib. But I felt for him. It was a proud – and pathetic – attempt to convince us that he's getting on with his life – a normal life. Obviously he isn't. Sad."

"I'll believe he's in the clear if DNA evidence rules him out."

Clare was not optimistic. "After five days in water? You'll be lucky to get any DNA that's not just Woodman's. I reckon you're going to have to crack this one without much forensic back-up. For once you're going to have to trust your feelings about suspects after you've talked to them. Not just scientific results." Clare enjoyed teasing him. "You talked about chasing devils. Now you're going to have to recognize them without getting some clever test done on their horns." She hesitated and then added thoughtfully, "When you said it, you didn't know that the victim was a devil himself."

Brett swallowed his mouthful of food and said, "What do you mean? That this time we're not looking for a devil who's killed an angel but an angel who's killed a devil?"

Clare tilted her head and raised her eyebrows in an expression that both questioned and answered positively.

"There's plenty of possible motives," Brett mused, "but you're assuming he was killed because of who he was, because of his conviction."

"Aren't you as well? He was hanged, Brett. Very judicial, very judgmental. It feels like a punishment – by someone who thought a prison sentence wasn't enough. The question is: who let on about his past?

And who received – and used – the information?"
She looked at the remains of Brett's mushroom pilau
and asked, "Have you gone completely vegetarian
now?"

"Meat is murder," he replied with a smile, "and
I'm innocent."

"Well, don't tell the squad," Clare advised him.
"They think you should have raw steak – and three
Weetabix – for breakfast."

Brett's mobile phone rang and several of the other
diners glared at him. "Yes?" he muttered quietly into
the phone.

It was Liz's voice. "I just found a report from
Grayson's supervisor in Sheffield Probation Service.
Guess what? Grayson missed his fortnightly check-
in. Didn't turn up. I wonder why not," she said
whimsically. "The Probation Service wanted police
back-up to trace his whereabouts."

"Did you enlighten them?" Brett asked.

"I assured the supervisor that he doesn't want to
see his client right now. Not a pretty sight. Told him
that Grayson's not likely to re-offend – not a danger
to the community any more." Liz paused and then
continued, "I've been a busy girl. Got a list of who
knew about Grayson. His name, description and
history were released to the local housing authority
and the heads of two schools – one in Oughtibridge,
the other in Worrall. Normal police procedure when
a registered abuser moves into a district."

"Thanks, Liz. When we get back, we'll go and

have words with them."

"I could go with someone right now. I've got their home addresses."

"No," Brett decided. "You work on the local press and Woodman's – Grayson's – circle of friends. That's the best thing you can do for the case at the moment."

Clare asked, "Do I gather Liz was offering to get out into the field again?"

Brett nodded as he put the phone away.

"She'd be good, you know. Remember the Jordan Loveday affair? She was spot-on, posing as a book collector. Did a job for us."

"I know. I agree. Just that we need her talent most in the incident room."

"Male DI chains female detective to computer," Clare murmured with a hint of both humour and gravity in her tone. "Not good for morale. Like a husband chaining wife to the kitchen sink."

"What is this? Women's Institute ganging up on poor harassed male detective?" Brett placed his fork across his empty plate. "When there's an opportunity, when it feels right, she'll get her chance."

When Clare had finished her meal, they headed for the Woodmans' house. It was small terraced property clad with aluminium at the front and constructed of wooden slats at the back. The roof was flat and, judging by the stains on the wallpaper, probably leaked in heavy weather. The interior walls appeared vulnerable to a determined shoulder barge.

Every movement in the houses on either side reverberated through the thin dividing walls into the Woodmans' cramped, dull and airless living room. The neighbours' conversations penetrated the walls as an indistinct murmur but their shouts and curses were perfectly audible. The room smelled of cigarette smoke and dogs. There was no sign of a dog but occasional bouts of barking outside, perhaps from the back garden, were plain.

Wiping into her cupped hand some ash that her husband's cigarette had deposited on the arm of the sofa, Mrs Woodman looked at Clare and said, "Yes. We know. Last night, a policewoman… She came out with it blunt like, but she was, you know, sympathetic."

"To be absolutely sure, Mrs Woodman, we'll have to get you up to Sheffield to identify him officially. I'm sorry."

"So the other policewoman said." She let out a breath. Ray Woodman's mother seemed regretful about her son's death but not shattered. His father just sat there on the couch, watching some television programme without the sound. Control in one hand and burning cigarette in the other, he was a silent immovable lump that Mrs Woodman tended like a worker bee.

Gently, Clare said, "And we've got to ask you a few questions because we're investigating Ray's death."

"He wasn't a bad boy," his mother claimed. "Not really. I know he hurt… But you know what I mean?

He didn't deserve… Deep down, he was good." She sank into a seat. "Perhaps it's for the best, though. He won't hurt anyone no more. I can look back on the good times without having to worry about … you know … if he's doing it again." She glanced up at the ceiling and added, "At least he's in a better place than jail."

Clare recognized a torn woman. Mrs Woodman was hiding a mother's grief, defending a flawed son, and taking comfort from the fact that he no longer tormented others. Clare asked her, "After he'd done his time, did he come back here?"

"Till they hounded him out."

"They?"

"It didn't take long. The local papers and folks with kids. They wouldn't leave him alone. Didn't want him living here, near their children. He had to get out and change his name."

Clare nodded. "Would any of them have followed him up north, do you think?"

Mrs Woodman shook her head. "Just wanted to get him out of here." While Mrs Woodman answered, Clare's eye flitted to a raw and blistered patch on her left arm. Quickly, Ray's mum covered it up with her other hand and explained, "Scalded myself. An accident with the kettle."

"Yes. Sure," Clare muttered wearily.

For the first time, Mr Woodman looked away from the TV screen. He scowled first at Clare and then at his wife. He was a big man with enormous rounded shoulders. His hairline was receding but his fair hair was cropped so close to his head that it was difficult to tell. From a distance, he would appear to be bald.

"What about you?" Clare asked him. "Do you know anyone who'd harm your son?" She could not quite keep the repugnance from her voice as she spoke to the architect of Ray Woodman's wrecked life.

Fussily, Mrs Woodman watched the lengthening grey stalk of her husband's cigarette. She avoided looking him in the face.

"No," he snapped. "The boy turned out no good. Had plenty of discipline but he still turned out no good. Got what was coming to him." Then he switched his attention back to the silent television.

Mrs Woodman made a dash for the precarious cylinder of ash at the end of his cigarette but, before she could slip her hand underneath it to catch it like an expert fielder, her husband shifted in his seat and the ash was dislodged prematurely on to the material of the sofa. Clare got the impression that he did it on purpose – to show that he had as much control over his wife as he had over the television.

Clare's job required her to be civil to this vile bully when really she wanted to get hold of him by the throat and make him admit that he had violated and tainted his own son. And that he was mistreating his downtrodden wife in an unattractive game of domestic domination.

Mrs Woodman looked up nervously and said hastily, "It wasn't Steve's fault."

It didn't matter to Clare whether Mrs Woodman was referring to the slovenly flick of cigarette ash or to the pollution of her son. Either way, she was so frightened of her husband that she lied.

Clare and Brett asked a few more questions but really they were wasting their time. The Woodmans had nothing to add to the inquiry and the longer Clare stayed inside their claustrophobic house, the more enraged she became.

Getting back into the car, she said to Brett, "Well, Steve Woodman didn't kill his son, that's for sure. He didn't care enough one way or the other to summon the effort." She snorted derisively. "He poisoned Ray's life. Handed down an inheritance of cruelty that Ray could pass on to others. Most abused kids don't go on to be abusers, I'm glad to say, but Steve Woodman left a legacy as powerful as DNA and genes. Ray couldn't resist it. It's all to do with control and being insecure and inadequate. Woodman – senior and then junior – made up for it by dominating someone weaker than themselves. That way they feel important."

"Till someone else ends their reign of terror," Brett remarked. Relieved, he accelerated away from the Woodmans' house.

CaseCall had never had such an easy task. Tom Grayson had made so few telephone calls in his time at Oughtibridge that the intelligence programme could not compile a worthwhile map of contacts. He had called only his parents, the electricity company, the benefits office and Pete's Pizzas. A sparse circle of friends. The local newspapers had not run any stories on him so his true identity and his record of abusing children had not leaked out that way – if it had at all. Inquiries around town had drawn a blank. Either he kept himself to himself or his neighbours were keeping their thoughts to themselves. The people in the town had glanced at his photograph, pushed out their bottom lips, shook their heads and denied seeing or knowing him. Only one shopkeeper recognized him as a person who'd been in her store a few times. He'd bought only basic items – and the cheapest varieties. She knew nothing about him.

Quizzing Liz, Brett asked, "No job, I suppose?"

"On the dole," she answered. "A record for messing with kids doesn't make for an uplifting and attractive CV. This is one sad cookie," Liz declared. "But we've probably got the boat that took him out on to the reservoir. They got some blood in one of the rowing boats. Too early to confirm it's Grayson's. And only a tiny amount, apparently. I suppose that means the body had dripped its last drop, the boat was scrubbed down afterwards or he was bagged pretty effectively."

Brett nodded. "But it does mean the vehicle that took him from the cottage to the reservoir might also have a drop or two. Worth remembering for later."

"The rowing boat belongs to one Jamie Lennox. I did a bit of sniffing around in data – since that's the only thing I know how to do," she added pointedly. "Late thirties. Lives in Oughtibridge. Church-goer because one of the team doing the rounds of the churches last Sunday interviewed him. Nothing worth reporting but the officer who talked to him said he seemed fidgety."

"Fidgety," Brett repeated. "Probably been sitting for too long on a hard pew."

When Brett stopped the car outside the Oughtibridge shops, there was a welcoming party waiting for him.

As soon as he emerged, a delighted retriever, tail wagging enthusiastically, met him on the pavement. Brett shook his head and smiled. "I don't believe it!" He patted the dog's head.

"It's nice to know that someone loves you: your pesky pal," Clare said with a cheerful smirk. "If you didn't want a canine friend, you shouldn't have fed him."

They strode up the hill to Poplar Road where Ray Woodman, with his new name of Tom Grayson, had found cheap rented accommodation. Behind them on Church Street, tyres screeched and a car sounded its horn. Strolling dangerously across the road behind the detectives, the retriever ignored the irate driver. Brett turned and said, "You'll get yourself run over. Why don't you go home?"

The dog did not pay any attention. It went up to Grayson's front door, sat and whined loudly. "Strange reaction," Clare murmured to herself.

A neighbour appeared on his doorstep and exclaimed, "That dog! What a pain! It's always hanging around."

The man was talking aloud to himself, not to Brett, but Brett took the opportunity to shout, "He doesn't live here, then?"

"No, pal. It doesn't," he snorted. "Belongs to an old man down the bottom end of the village. Puts it out to find for itself – and feed itself – all day. This week it's taken to getting into the bins. Whoever was feeding it before must have stopped."

Clare glanced at Brett. They were both thinking the same thing: perhaps Tom Grayson had been the retriever's benefactor. Perhaps the dog had been with Grayson when he'd been taken to be hanged. The retriever could be their best, yet silent, witness.

When they approached the neighbour and showed him their IDs, he groaned. "Not again!" He didn't invite them inside.

"The dog," Brett began. "Has he been around here much in the last month?"

"Yeah. He's been all over the village for the last year. Pest!"

"Did Tom Grayson next door feed him, do you know?"

He shrugged uncooperatively. "No idea. I suppose someone round here must have."

"I know some officers have already spoken to you—"

"Twice," he interrupted.

"Did you know anything about Mr Grayson next door? What kind of man he was?"

The resident shrugged. "A very private one. Hardly saw him."

"I've only got one more question," Brett announced. "Last Thursday night, maybe in the early hours of Friday, did you see a large car, van or truck here?"

"Can't say I did, no."

"Any other activity that night?"

"I was asleep."

"All right," Brett replied. "Just to let you know, in case you hear any noise, we're going into Grayson's house for a bit."

"Please yourselves," the man responded tersely. He went back inside and closed the door a little too hurriedly.

They got the same unhelpful response from all of the nearby residents, who seemed to resent the police disrupting their normally quiet and isolated lives. Clare and Brett gave up and, keeping the retriever outside, entered Grayson's last home instead. It wasn't much: a loose collection of odd furnishings and fittings. Cheapness came before comfort or refinement. While Brett looked around, Clare called the Woodmans. She was relieved when Ray Woodman's mother answered the phone rather than his father. Presumably Steve didn't have the energy or the will to pick up a ringing telephone. He would leave it to his wife. "Sorry to bother you again, Mrs Woodman," Clare said, "but did Ray like dogs?"

Mrs Woodman hesitated, probably surprised by the unexpected question. Then she answered, "Like them? He loved them. When he was little, you know, he had a pet. Just a mongrel but Ray loved it. Slept in his room, licked his face, whined when Ray got hurt. But it ... had an accident. Poor little thing. It died, I'm afraid."

An accident. Clare assumed it was like Mrs Woodman's accident with the boiling water. The sort of accident that only happened when Steve

Woodman was nearby. "Thanks, Mrs Woodman. It's probably nothing but, you never know, it might be helpful."

Brett came back into the living room and reported, "The windows at the back are boarded-up, but nothing else unusual. No sign of a struggle. Still, I want the support group to give it a good going over. And Forensics. Let's see if the dog came in here – and if the rug's got any traces from other people's shoes."

"The case of the hungry hound," Clare mused. "Sounds like Sherlock Holmes."

Brett smiled and nodded. "Pity our only possible witness so far is a dog."

"You don't relish putting him on the stand in court, then?"

"Too easy to bribe," Brett declared. "A pound of steak and he'd testify to anything."

While they were in the area, they walked through the village to interview the head of the local school. It was a gorgeous day, clear, hot and sunny. Bearing a good tan, Brett welcomed it. As pink as a well-cooked shrimp, Clare dodged the sunlight as much as possible by striding from shadow to shadow. Halfway to the headteacher's house, the dog fell behind, captivated by smells, and lost interest in the detectives. Clare and Brett did not see their fickle canine companion again that day.

The headteacher told them that, towards the end of term, she had put the school on yellow alert for a while. Staff on playground duty had kept an eye open for a man like Grayson but none of them had seen anyone loitering anywhere near the school. And, no, she had not shown his photograph to anyone in the local community. It was exactly the same story from the head of the school down the road in Worral.

There were two more visits to be made before the end of the working week. Tom Grayson's supervisor in the probation service shook his head ruefully. "It's a pity. I hardly knew the man but … I had a feeling about him. And his notes from Bucks were hopeful."

"In what way?" Clare queried.

"With these chaps, abusers, they don't see they've done anything wrong. They don't accept that their behaviour with youngsters is … inappropriate. In fact they're often quite articulate, finding clever arguments to defend their abuse. If they don't believe they're doing wrong, they'll do it again. But I got the impression with Grayson that he was sorry. No clever-dick arguments. Not clever at all. Just after a new start, he said. I had some hopes he meant it. Some hopes he was a reformed character."

Clare was immensely saddened. If Tom had been hunted and executed by some self-appointed protector of Oughtibridge society, the vigilante had chosen a man who had done his time, paid for his crimes and resolved to change. The supervisor's opinion was consistent with her view of the threatening letters sent to Nathan Shaw. She did not believe for a moment that Ray Woodman had sent them.

Someone in Milton Keynes was plaguing Nathan and hiding under Woodman's name.

The local housing authority was used to dealing with offenders in the community. It was used to handling sensitive information from the police on the settlement of released prisoners. Their internal system, where information was seen by staff only on a need-to-know basis, was more secure than the police's own procedures. Brett thought that a leak was unlikely. Even so, he took the names of all workers who knew about Tom Grayson's history and new location.

In the evening, Clare and Brett visited Jamie Lennox back in Oughtibridge. He was doing well for himself. He owned one of the larger properties in the wooded outskirts of the village, not far from the abandoned cottage. The lane to his house was a quiet single-track road made of loose stone. Leading up to his front door and garage he had a newly laid drive-way of expensive block paving. Lennox was single and lived on his own but, Clare and Brett observed, the dining room was set up for two people to have dinner together. Brett also noticed that there were no wine glasses on the table. He wondered if Jamie Lennox was teetotal.

"Yes," Jamie was saying, "I've got a couple of boats on Damflask. A rowing boat – I don't use it much nowadays – and a yacht."

"Have you used the rowing boat in the last couple of weeks?" asked Brett.

"No. Why?"

Brett decided to be open and watch for a reaction. "We think it's been used to transport a body."

Apparently trying to convince himself that the whole thing was not a bad dream, Jamie stared at Brett. "Really? That's…" he struggled for a word, "…dreadful. Who'd…?"

"That's what we're trying to find out," Brett put in.

"This body. Who?"

Brett did not want to explain or identify Tom Grayson yet. "We're working on it."

Jamie looked concerned. He turned to one side and snatched a glance at his watch. "Sorry," he mumbled. "I'm expecting … a friend."

"We won't be much longer," Brett told him. "Do you know anything about the burnt cottage up the road?"

Jamie was taken aback by the sudden switch. "No. It's not far from here but you can't see it. I smelled burning one night but I thought it was a bonfire. Someone burning rubbish." He seemed keen to deny any involvement.

"Do you have a job, Mr Lennox?" Brett enquired.

"Yes. I'm a butcher."

"A butcher," Brett repeated softly. Then he said, "I noticed you've got a big workshop out the back. Have you got a hacksaw?"

Jamie's brow creased. "Yes."

"It hasn't disappeared recently?"

"No. I used it yesterday, actually. Why…?"

Brett interrupted, saying, "Well, if you've got company, we'd better leave you to it. I'm afraid we've impounded your boat for a few days."

Jamie shrugged. "It's not important. I hope you ... get your man. I don't like the idea of some psycho running round here."

On the doorstep, Brett said, "One final thing. Have you seen a retriever roaming around up here?"

"Seen him? I've nearly run him over twice."

On leaving, they passed a woman coming in the opposite direction. She turned into the narrow lane and then into Jamie's driveway. Immediately, Clare used the radio to ask Liz for vehicle identification. Clare reeled off the registration number of the woman's car.

It took Liz only thirty seconds. "Laura Magnall," she announced. "Resident of Oughtibridge."

"Thanks, Liz," Clare replied. "Laura Magnall," she murmured aloud. "A familiar name."

"Yes," Brett agreed as he waited to turn right into Langsett Road. "Chelsea Magnall. Mentioned as a girl who went to the cottage sometimes."

"Interesting, isn't it?" Clare said.

"Interesting profession Lennox has got, as well," Brett observed. "That means he knows how to handle meat, he's got access to vans, no doubt, and he'd know how to scrub down and bleach blood stains."

11

It was Friday evening. Clare and Brett had to report to John that the first day of August, and the first week of the investigation, had passed disappointingly without an arrest. They had made a lot of progress but they had not unlocked the secrets of Oughtibridge. Back in the incident room, Brett said, "Liz, I've got a list of the people at the housing authority who knew Tom Grayson was Ray Woodman. And there's the two headteachers. Run them through your system and check if any have been victims of child abuse – or have children or other relatives who might've been. Anything that might cause a grudge against abusers like Tom Grayson. Anything that would make them want to get their own back by leaking details on Grayson and his offences."

"Brett," Liz replied quietly, "you're forgetting

something. Something else you should get me to check. You can't turn a blind eye to it. An internal check. Any police officer who might hate abusers."

Brett nodded and sighed. He regretted that it was necessary to assess his own colleagues. "I know," he agreed. "You're right. Go ahead. But be discreet, Liz. I don't want everyone to know we're contemplating a leak so close to home."

"Oh, I don't know," Liz retorted. "There's some testosterone-ridden officers I'd like to nail."

Before the end of the day, Brett examined the most recent e-mails from the forensic department. There were several reports and three caught his eye. Two confirmed the identity of the victim. Blood from the body washed up at Damflask Reservoir matched the details in Ray Woodman's criminal profile. And the teeth matched Woodman's dental record. Brett was relieved that the forensic work had not thrown up any nasty surprises or complications. The third report was more revealing. The electron microscope had not detected any adhesives near the mouth or wrists but it had spotted several traces near the bottom of both trouser legs. X-ray analysis of the spots had measured the characteristic elements making up the glue. Comparison of the results with a database identified an adhesive that was composed exactly of those elements. It was used on Manco duct tape.

Over a coffee, Clare asked Brett, "What's on the cards tomorrow, then? Saturday, but not a day off."

For a moment, an ironic grin appeared on Brett's face.

"What is it?" Clare enquired curiously.

"Nothing," Brett answered. Then he admitted, "Actually, it's my birthday. Second of August. Two years off the big three-o."

Clare laughed. "Nearly ancient. Past it. Retirement beckons. But, before that, you've got to celebrate, case or not. I'll treat you to a lemonade or two. It'll be good. Take our minds off it for a bit."

"Thanks," Brett replied. "Sounds good. But, for the first time in years my mum and dad have invited me to spend the day – or some of it – with them. I can't let them down, not after what they've been through." He paused and then said, "I don't suppose you'd… No. Forget it."

"I don't think it's a good idea, Brett," she said, guessing the remainder of his question. "They might get the wrong impression. Besides, I've got to go and get my arm looked at. Show off my war wound to some nurse."

"Before we go off to parents and nurses, we'd better chase the duct tape. Just a quick look in Pillinger's shop for starters."

Clare was tired but not too tired. That night she went out for food and a film with friends from the karate club before settling down with a book and a favourite ale. She would regret the late night in the morning but that was hours away. She had to take the

100

time to wind down before going to bed. She wanted to sink into sleep thinking about a novel, poetry, a painting. She did not want to be kept awake by crazed crooks and hideous crimes.

In the morning, she got up later than she intended and had to skimp on breakfast to be ready when Brett arrived in the car. Her arm ached. In the night, she must have been lying on the wound. While she dashed around the house, preparing herself, she thought of Brett. Her partner would have been up and out for an early-morning run or swim ages ago. The man was a saint or a madman. Clare's biological clock was set to a different time zone. She was a late-night person.

Clambering into the car alongside Brett, she mumbled, "Morning." Brett looked fresh, clean-shaven, showered and raring to go. His broad shoulders filled the driver's seat. His dark hair was cut short and smelled faintly of shampoo. She had to admit it: Brett was the sort of man most women would want their boyfriend to look like. Physically strong, strong features, strong on compassion. And she knew that his reputation for being a little cold was only reputation: it came from his cool scientific examination of cases. But several times Clare had seen him weakened by emotion. She had been touched by his distress. "You know," she said as she snapped shut her seat belt, "I could get used to having a chauffeur."

"After the nurse has given you the all-clear today,

there's no excuse. You'll be back in the driving seat," Brett said.

"Yes, sir," Clare replied with mock humility. "I know my place. After all, I'm a lowly and unworthy DS. And a member of Help the Aged. Happy birthday!"

Oughtibridge was quiet. Outside Jeff Pillinger's shop, though, there was a small van with its rear doors open. Clare and Brett lingered at the back of the vehicle and looked inside. Down the centre were laid bundles of copper tubing. Along the sides there was a jumble of stock items. A stepladder, still wrapped in cellophane, was propped against the back of the driver's seat. There was nothing to suggest that the van had once carried a mutilated corpse.

Pillinger came out and, surprised to see the detectives watching him restocking his shop, muttered hurriedly, "All legit. Nothing off the back of a lorry. All recognized makes."

Brett grinned. "Not my line of business," he said. "You could walk in with a load of stolen goods and I wouldn't recognize them."

"Ah, that's right," Pillinger retorted. "You're into the heavy stuff, aren't you? Arson and murder." He leaned into the van, grabbed a bunch of pipes, clutched them under his right arm and, in his left hand, took some saws. When he turned round, he nearly speared the officers on the end of the ducting.

Clare and Brett stepped back and then followed Pillinger into his shop which was devoid of customers. "Arson, yes," Brett remarked. "But who said anything about murder?"

For an instant, Pillinger paused and then he laughed. He balanced the pipes across the counter and said, "Oh, come on! It's all over the village – and have you seen the local paper? You come in here asking me about rope, you dredge up a body, you saturate the place with cops asking about a missing chap. Word up on Poplar Close is that it's a bloke called Grayson."

"Did you know him?" asked Clare.

"Can't say I did. New arrival, they say."

"And what's the word on what sort of bloke he was?"

Pillinger shrugged and looked away. "No one seems to know," he muttered.

"Just one thing," Brett put in. "Duct tape."

"Sure," Jeff replied. "Over there – adhesives and tape." He pointed to the left-hand wall.

Brett strolled over and glanced at Pillinger's stock. He selected a roll of Manco duct tape and took it to the counter. "Anyone else bought any of this stuff recently?" he enquired.

"Not that I remember." Pillinger held out his hand for Brett's money. "Why are you taking it? Home work or detective work?"

"Birthday present," Brett answered, enjoying a private joke with Clare.

Pillinger cast a sidelong glance at Brett and said, "Did you measure up that plasterboard you wanted?"

Without a hint of hesitation, Brett smiled and said, "The police officer's life is a busy one. No, sorry. No sale yet."

Before she got back into the car, Clare eyed the village shop and said to Brett, "I'll be with you in a second." She jogged across the road. When she returned, she twisted in her seat and held out a gift to Brett: a heavily iced and decorated Sheffield Wednesday birthday cake. "Many happy returns – and I bet you half of it that Pillinger's our man."

Brett chuckled with pleasure. "Mmm. Choice health food," he joked. "Thanks. But what makes you think I'd risk half a good cake on a dodgy bet? What's your evidence against him?"

Clare tapped the side of her nose.

"Not your policewoman's intuition again!" Brett exclaimed. "I come up with theories that are just as wild – maybe more so – but at least there's a few facts behind them."

"True," Clare admitted, "but *I* have the knack of getting it right. Pillinger's got all the tools and he's cagey, suspicious."

In good humour Brett mocked, "M'Lord, the defendant's guilty because he looks funny."

Clare laughed. "Yeah. I know. But even so…"

On Sunday Clare did start driving again. The fresh dressing on her arm was much lighter than the previous one and the extra freedom of movement felt liberating. The newly unveiled skin was white in contrast with the freckled red of the rest of her arm. Carefully avoiding the wound, she had rubbed more sun screen into the pale patch than into the darker skin that had been exposed to the brutal sunlight all along.

"How's it doing?" Brett enquired, nodding towards her arm.

"Model patient, me. Healing nicely, I'm told."

"Good," Brett said. "That means I can leave any rough stuff to you."

"Thanks," Clare replied, her tone overflowing with sarcasm. "How were your folks, anyway? Where are they living now?"

"I tried to persuade them north – somewhere like Edale. They'd like it. But… I guess it's hard at their age when they've always lived in Kent. They've stayed down there. Same town, just moved out of a rented place into a house of their own. You know, we spent the day avoiding talking about my sister," Brett said quietly. "But, for the first time, I got the impression that it's on the cards. When they're settled, when they feel the new bungalow is really home, then we'll talk. For now, it's more a matter of getting shelves up, the kitchen fitted and new furniture sorted out."

"Not the best weather for lugging furniture about."

"It *was* hot and sweaty."

"Any plasterboard or duct tape work?" Clare asked with a grin.

"Very funny," Brett muttered.

It was almost a disappointment that they were not met in Poplar Close by the freerange retriever. They went straight to Chelsea Magnall's house where they interviewed the fifteen-year-old in the presence of her mother, Laura. As usual when they dealt with young people, Clare took the lead.

Once Chelsea had denied being at the cottage on the night of the blaze, or knowing anything about the fire, Clare said, "We've got the word of several boys that you and Deborah Pillinger used to go to the cottage. Is that right?"

While Chelsea faltered, wondering whether to admit to it, Clare glanced at her mother. Laura's face told Clare immediately that the testimony had not come as a shock to her. She knew that her daughter had frequented the derelict cottage.

Eventually, Chelsea nodded. "Not a lot but, yes, sometimes."

"What went on up there, Chelsea?"

Chelsea did not have the bravado of her friend, Debs. "This and that," she answered with bowed head. Her long mousy hair fell either side of her face, hiding it almost completely.

"Like?" Clare prompted.

"Nothing … bad."

"Remember, we've talked to a lot of your mates who went there. We'd like to hear your version."

The girl's mother encouraged her. "I'm sure you've got nothing to be ashamed of, Chelsea. Tell them."

"All right." Chelsea looked up and brushed her hair back. "You see, Debs goes out with one of the lads. Josh Redgrave. She met him, with his mates, at the cottage sometimes. Asked me to go with her. Some of them smoked, kicked a ball about. Josh and Debs … you know … hung out. I think she was trying to get me off with one of Joshua's mates but I didn't fancy him."

"It all sounds very innocent. You ought to have seen what I got up to at your age." Clare smiled at a memory. "So why be coy about it? I think there was something else. Tell me about it."

Chelsea looked briefly at her mother and then stammered, "Well, there was this boy. Moved away from Oughtibridge now. He was … worse than Josh. Broke into a couple of houses round here. People got fed up with it but they – adults – didn't know who was doing it. We did. He was ruining everything. Giving everyone grief. Especially Josh. Because Josh has got a bad name for himself, everyone thought it was him. But it wasn't," Chelsea said. "One day, Josh and his mates got hold of this lad and took him to the cottage. He'd even got a cassette player with him that he'd nicked. They smashed his tape and returned the machine."

"Is that all?" Clare enquired, expecting that Chelsea had left out the vital part.

"Well," she admitted, "they roughed him up a bit."

"A bit?"

"Maybe more than a bit, but he was OK. He walked away after."

Clare nodded. "I see. When was this?"

"Oh, we were still at school. Last month."

Clare's brain struggled to keep focused when images of her own attack on Adrian Telfer came to mind. Years ago, he had knifed her dad and stolen a Walkman from him. For a moment last week, despite her training, Clare felt an uncontrollable urge for vengeance. She *could* have flattened him. How could *she* criticize Joshua Redgrave and the other boys? They were protecting their own reputations and their community. While Clare understood the boys' behaviour, the law – and DS Tilley – had to condemn it. "All right, Chelsea," Clare said. "I don't think this has got anything to do with our inquiry, but you'd better tell me the lad's name, his injuries, and who was there – just in case."

"I won't get anyone into trouble?"

"I don't think so. I assume the boy didn't go to the local police and complain so it's not our business. We can't approve of anyone taking the law into their own hands, Chelsea, but it seems this one's over and done with." After noting down all of the details that Chelsea could remember or was willing to give, Clare asked, "Do you know a man called Tom Grayson? Lives just round the corner. Forty-odd years old, single." She looked at Laura and added, "Either of you."

Both of them shook their heads.

Clare held out his photograph. Chelsea studied it and then said, "Definitely not."

Laura barely looked at the photograph – as if it would hurt her eyes.

"Well?" Clare urged, unwilling to let Chelsea's mother off the hook.

"It's the one who was killed at the cottage, isn't it?" Laura winced. "That's what people have been saying."

"Do you know him? Know anything about him?"

"Horrible," she said with a shiver. "No, I don't."

"Is there a Mr Magnall who we could speak to as well?" Clare enquired.

"Single mum," Laura replied.

"OK," said Clare. "That's it for now. We may well need to speak to you again." While she said it, she looked at Laura Magnall.

In the car, Clare turned to Brett and queried, "Did you spot it? Laura's slip?"

"Like a sore thumb. Couldn't miss it."

"It could've just been educated guesswork. We've been out – and the team's been out – asking about the cottage, and folk round here have heard a body's turned up in the reservoir. On top of that she probably talked to Lennox about the questions we asked him on Friday night. She's put two and two together and come up with a murder in the cottage – something we've never mentioned to anyone."

Brett nodded. "Agreed. But it's still suspicious. *We've* still not confirmed Grayson copped it in the cottage. All we've got is a bit of rope there and we know he was hanged. It's *likely* he was killed there but we don't know for certain. It's interesting that Laura Magnall *does* seem to know."

"Could be pure speculation," Clare suggested. "Not everyone's as exact as you are. A lot of people say things and sound definite when really they're not sure. Guesswork comes out as fact. Rumour gets repeated as the truth. Maybe that's all it is."

"Could be," Brett agreed, "but what about the important stuff? What *did* you get up to when you were fifteen?"

"I was just bonding with the girl," Clare responded evasively. "Sympathetic interviewing technique. It's called acting, Brett."

"Sure," he replied cynically. "I'll have to use my imagination."

"Where to now?" Clare asked.

"My place, of course," Brett replied. "You've got to help me finish off a cake."

"Good, is it?"

"You'll put pounds on. I'll work it off on the squash court."

12

"**Y**ou've got yourself a witness, Brett," Liz boomed across the room on Monday.

Hopeful, both Clare and Brett made for Liz who, as always, was transfixed by the computer.

She pointed to her monitor and explained, "Forensic's got retriever hairs on the carpet in Grayson's front room."

"Man's best friend," Clare interjected.

"He would be if he could talk," Brett replied. "Makes me think, though. If our doggy friend tried to protect his main source of food, he might've nipped anyone who went for Grayson. Remember?"

Clare thought about it for a moment and then announced, "Deborah Pillinger – with the injured hand."

"It's a possibility." Turning back to Liz, Brett asked, "Anything else from Grayson's place?"

"No fingerprints that aren't Grayson's – or Woodman's, whichever way you put it. A bit of mud that's dropped out of someone's tread, probably Grayson's own shoe, they reckon. A few human hairs but they could belong to the previous occupants. Glass fragments in the back room showing the windows were broken from the outside. No photos of local kids or anything like that. The place isn't teeming with evidence."

"Told you," Clare said to Brett. "It's more about people than clues."

Sitting by Liz and keeping his voice down, Brett enquired, "Got anything on leaks?"

"Nowt. I couldn't find any records of child abuse in those headteachers, local authority staff or police – or their immediate families. None of them's known to have suffered. No obvious grudges," Liz concluded. "But you can't be sure." She paused before continuing in an affected whisper, "I did find out something, though. As someone called B. Lawless, you'll appreciate this. I found a DS in Fraud called Robin Banks."

Brett groaned theatrically. "Not our man. Keep your eye open for A. Butcher. He's the one we want." More seriously, he added, "There *is* something you could check on. Grayson was bound with strong sticky tape. How many DIY places around here sell Manco duct tape?"

"OK."

"No DNA results back yet?"

"You've got to be kidding!" Liz exploded. "There's a huge backlog at the lab where they do it. On your authority, and being a murder case, I've got our samples pushed in near the front of the queue but there's still a wait."

Frustrated, Brett said forcibly, "Right. I want the team back out on the streets. Let's question every member of the rowing and yachting clubs. We only need one of them to indulge in moonlit frolics by the reservoir and we might get some useful stuff. I want a roadside survey through the night as well. Stop anyone who uses the roads around Damflask. See if they drove there on the night of the twenty-fourth, twenty-fifth. Include Calum Laidlow in that. See if he saw anything when he was driving around that night. And I don't care if we've spoken to everyone living between Grayson's place and the cottage, do it again. This time get the team to ask specifically about *any* vehicle they saw on the night of the fire. If we get any hits at all, move Forensics in with the best blood detection tests they've got." He turned to Clare and added, "OK, let's do it your way for a bit – at least till we get those DNA tests through."

The retriever was standing outside The King's Arms, staring at the door of the pub. At the sound of two car doors opening and closing in the parking lane outside the shops, the dog turned and galloped across the road. Luckily, there was no traffic. He hurtled up to Brett, nuzzling his hand expectantly.

Clare thought that Brett was about to grumble that the dog was a nuisance but he didn't. He hesitated as if struck by a sudden idea – possibly a crazy idea – and then knelt down. He fiddled with the dog's collar and then, with a smile, said to Clare, "Relatively clever dog. Name of Einstein."

On hearing his name, the dog gazed quizzically at Brett.

"Still hungry," Clare guessed. "I don't think you'll ever convert *him* into a vegetarian."

Brett went into the shop, bought a large sausage roll, and gave it to Einstein on the pavement.

Clare shook her head. "You're spoiling him. We'll never get rid of him now."

"Let's get going before he polishes it off. Besides," Brett added mysteriously, "I might want him to return the favour sometime."

In the Health Centre, they eventually got to see the nurse who had tended to Deborah Pillinger's damaged hand. Cleverly, Clare insisted that, because they already knew about Deborah's injury and it was minor, patient confidentiality was not an issue. Under her pressure, the nurse agreed and mentioned that he had also given Deborah a tetanus jab.

"When was this?" asked Clare.

The nurse looked at his notes and said, "The twenty-fifth. Friday morning."

Clare glanced at Brett and then enquired, "Was it a bad cut?"

"Not really. To be sure, I put a stitch in the biggest, deepest one but, no, it wasn't bad."

"There was more than one cut, then?"

The nurse held out his own hand and drew a straight line across it. "A row of punctures."

Clare's eyebrows rose. "Could it have been a bite? Teeth marks?"

"I wouldn't have thought so," he answered. "That would be a curved pattern, wouldn't it? Deborah said she caught it on the jagged glass of a broken window. Being straight, it seemed likely."

"You didn't ask how she did it?"

"It's my job to patch people up, not to play cops and robbers."

"All right," Clare concluded. "You're building up a queue of patients so we'd better let you get on. Thanks. You've been very helpful."

The teacher who took Joshua, Debs and Laura for RE was at the school, working on her schedule for next year. They interviewed her in a classroom that had seen better days. Paint was peeling from the wall underneath the leaky window and the broken blinds failed to keep out the fierce sunlight. Clare was forced to squint until she positioned herself with her back to the window. The shadows of the blinds sliced across the teacher's body. Clare did not reveal the precise nature of the crime that they were investigating. Instead she explained, "We just want to get a feel for some of your pupils – and their parents perhaps. We think you'll be able to help put us in the picture."

"You were thinking of specific students?"

"I could name a few, I suppose, but not particularly, no. In general, how would you sum up the attitude of your kids – the fifteen-year-olds – to moral issues like crime and punishment? You must cover it in RE."

"You're well-informed," the teacher replied. "Yes. We covered it last year, along with euthanasia and capital punishment."

"And?"

"And I suppose they surprised me on the whole. I've been in this crazy profession for nearly thirty years and over that time I've got used to kids being reasonably liberal," she responded. "But recently, with career, self and money in the driving seat, I've noticed a hardening. Especially here in Oughtibridge. A lot of them were quite punitive – very much an-eye-for-an-eye attitude. Certainly capital punishment didn't get the thumbs down from the majority."

"Do these views come from their parents, do you think, or do the students themselves form their own opinions?"

"There's no one answer to that. It depends. Most of them deserve a lot of credit. More than they get, anyway. They think for themselves. Better now than in my schooldays, I'll tell you. Don't you believe all that nonsense about falling standards. But there's always a bit of gang culture – the views held in fear of being at odds with the mass. There's a bit of follow-my-leader as well, where they adopt the opinion of one outspoken person who they look up to. And there are just a few kids whose views are the same as the last person they spoke to. On the whole, though, they're pretty good at jostling for their own position."

"What about Joshua Redgrave?"

"One of the leaders. A tough nut."

"Deborah Pillinger?"

"Another member of the hang-'em-high brigade. Maybe she gets it from Josh – a thing going with him, you know – or her family or from within herself. I don't know."

"And Chelsea Magnall?"

"Sweet girl, but tends to be overawed by Debs. I know her mother, Laura. Not the most robust or decisive woman. She's … I hope I don't put my foot in it here … she's old-fashioned feminine, so you know where Chelsea's coming from. Not a pushy girl."

"Thanks," Clare said, rising from her seat. "I'm sorry I can't tell you exactly what this is all about but your comments have helped. We won't bother you any more."

"You're welcome," the teacher responded with a smile. "The school feels eerie without the kids. Heaven, actually. But it's nice to break the silence sometimes. Otherwise I begin to think I can hear their ghosts haunting me."

Clare tried the same theme with one of the vicars, Reverend Hughes. In fact, she was tempted to linger over her interview with him because his room in the church was airy and cool. "What's the mood of your parishioners to law and order, would you say?"

"They have every respect for the law but they also recognize that there's a higher authority. I encourage them to live by Christian law."

"And how would you sum that up?" Clare asked him. "Love thy neighbour or an eye for an eye?"

Reverend Hughes paused. He thought that he sensed a touch of cynicism in Clare's tone but he decided to give her the benefit of the doubt. "They live *good* lives. Love for their fellows comes first."

"And what if they discovered they had a very bad person among them? Are any of them capable of taking a sinner out and stoning him?"

The vicar took a sharp breath. "No one is beyond redemption. In my sermons, I talk about the need for tolerance and forgiveness."

"I'm told not all your colleagues are so ... understanding."

"That may be so, Sergeant Tilley, but none of us are equipped to be judges. I would hope that people leave the stonings to those who are without sin."

Clare nodded. "Yes, I see. But I'm asking you what you think they'd do, not what they *should* do."

"Look," he answered, "there may be a tendency these days to judge others a little too readily and harshly. Perhaps we're all guilty of that, even the police. But if you're asking me if I believe one of my congregation is capable of committing murder with their own hands – for whatever cause – then I'd have to say … I doubt it."

"What about Oughtibridge folk who aren't among your congregation?" asked Clare. "The ones who don't come to church."

"I can't speak for them," the vicar replied. "Obviously I'm not so … familiar with them. But I'd like to think they're good people."

On the surface, Clare had not learned a great deal from Reverend Hughes but he was very touchy on the topic of punishment and cautious in his claims for the residents. That meant he had his worries or suspicions – even if he was not prepared to speak against anyone.

In the church grounds, standing on the attractive criss-cross pattern of grey and reddish-brown block paving, Brett took a call on his mobile phone and patted Einstein at the same time. Liz told him, "Two DIY shops in Sheffield stock your manky duct tape, Brett."

"Manco."

"Whatever. It's not that hard to get hold of or unique to the Oughtibridge shop."

"Pity," he muttered. "Thanks, anyway." To Clare, he said, "Well? Do you still think people round here know more than they'll say?"

"Definitely," she answered.

"OK. I believe you. Let's go back to HQ and try something."

I n Surveillance, Brett explained the nature of their inquiry and then said to a technician called Deepak, "We've been told a few times that the whole village is talking about it. But not when *we* ask. And the pub goes quiet when a stranger walks in. You know the type. In cop shows they call it a wall of silence. I'd like to know what they're saying when we're not around. Now, there's a dog..."

Interrupting, Deepak said with a wry grin, "I can feel something unlikely coming on."

Brett carried on regardless. "Is it possible to attach a bug to the dog's collar and have someone stationed discreetly in the town, listening in and taping for me?"

"Taping what? Barking, scratching and chomping noises?"

"This dog wanders all over the place. I know we'll only get snatches of conversation – we may not know where he is exactly and who's speaking. But I'd settle for that. I want the words first. Who says them can come second."

Deepak sighed. "I've never done it before but…"

Brett smiled. "I know you'll enjoy the challenge."

"And how do we place the bug?"

"Einstein – that's the dog – is my mate," Brett explained. "At least, I've bribed him into being friendly. I'll lure him somewhere quiet and do it myself."

"And who'll run after him and put the wire back on if he has a good scratch at his neck and collar?" asked Deepak.

"I'll take a chance he hasn't got fleas."

"Good old foot-slogging police work didn't last long with you, did it?" Clare commented. "You're always thinking of short cuts and technology."

"Why slog around and get no results when you can get a hi-tech dog to do it for you and maybe produce the goods?"

"You just didn't give it long enough. No patience. Besides, I bet Einstein doesn't go in the pub – where you'd most like him. Where most of the chatting will go on." Clare explained, "Remember? When we went there before, he stopped outside and barked."

"I know," Brett replied. "Probably means nothing but … that's interesting, isn't it? Anyway, we'll just have to hope he wanders somewhere useful to us. Surely during a day or two he'll overhear something. Especially if he's hanging around the shops. That's the sort of place locals might bump into each other and talk. Like the DIY store. You'll thank me if Einstein catches your chief suspect nattering to someone about Grayson. Or our four-legged friend might go to Poplar Close again. Maybe he'll spot a gathering on a street corner and go up to them because he's friendly or hungry. No one's going to stop talking because a dog makes an entrance."

"OK, Brett. You've convinced me. A long shot but it's worth a try. You did pretty well with a wired cockroach last time; perhaps you can repeat it with a retriever." Slowing down for some red traffic lights, Clare glanced at him with a grin and said, "Obviously you're not against animal experiments."

Brett knew that his partner wasn't being serious but he answered her anyway. "It depends. If they get hurt, I am. But Einstein won't come to any harm because of this. No one's going to find out."

In Oughtibridge, Clare parked outside the café in the spot that seemed to have become reserved for police vehicles. The surveillance officer called Adam drove past, carefully avoiding looking at Brett and Clare. He had been detailed to park unobtrusively round the corner in Coward Drive where the receiver would be well within range of the dog's movements.

At the crossroads, there was no sign of Einstein. Brett sighed and then suggested, "Let's see what the ale's like in The King's Arms. We'll take a window seat."

Their information about the pub was right. As soon as they walked through the door, the bar lapsed into silence. The walking bird's nest that was Carl Greenacre welcomed them and, while he poured their drinks, chirped, "How's it going, your case?"

Clare wondered what would happen if she sounded upbeat. She decided to try the experiment. "*Very* well," she stressed. "Very well indeed, thanks."

Concentrating on the pump in one hand and tilted glass in the other, Carl glanced sideways at the detectives. "Er ... glad to hear it. Made an arrest?"

"You'll know when we do," Clare replied. She paused to watch his reaction and then added, "News seems to spread quickly around here."

Carl had overfilled the glass – unusually for a bartender – and had to carry it very carefully towards his customers. Even so, he spilled a little. "Well," he murmured, "I'm sure it's the same in any smallish place. Folk will talk. It passes the time." Quickly recovering his composure, he grinned mischievously as he took their money.

Sitting at a table, Clare tapped the side of her glass and said, "Not good but not bad."

A huge lorry rumbled past on the main road. Three old ladies were standing on the corner, shrinking from the noise of the lorry that had interrupted their gossiping. Two boys on mountain bikes began the long haul up Church Street. Clare hoped to see

Einstein tramping behind them, glad to have an excuse to go on a walk, but he didn't show. Neither she nor Brett could enquire about the missing retriever because it would be suspicious. They had no choice but to wait and hope.

Inside the pub, the low murmur of conversation had resumed. Clare caught only one exchange. An irate fan of Yorkshire Cricket Club was moaning loudly about his team's performance. Clare imagined that if she sampled the chat at each table, and at the darts board, she would not hear a single word about the person they knew as Tom Grayson and the way he had been bowled out. Yet the locals would probably talk about nothing else as soon as she left with Brett. She was annoyed. She was convinced that these people around her were shielding the killer of a man who was probably trying to come to terms with his crime, better his behaviour and maybe even make amends.

"You know what I'd like to do?" she said quietly but firmly to Brett so that no one else could hear. "Pick on a suspect. Not Jeff Pillinger – he's too hard. Someone like Jamie Lennox or Laura Magnall – or even Reverend Hughes. Drag them downtown, lock them up for a bit and then question them till they crack."

"Good old-fashioned police work again," Brett murmured with a smile. "Maybe. But let's see what our mole and the DNA analysis tell us first. If we don't get anywhere, yes, we'll start to squeeze someone."

"There's even our local barman," she replied, nodding towards Greenacre. "Remember, he hesitated when we mentioned RW to him. Why? I don't know. But if he knew that Grayson had been killed, he'd have been surprised by us asking about RW. Anyway," she said, "we should be working on the weakest link we can find. Laura Magnall's top of my list."

"I think I've always understood why the squad admires you, Clare. Now I'm beginning to see why they're a bit scared of you as well."

"You know, you're the second person to tell me I'm scary. I don't think—"

Brett nodded subtly towards the crossroads and said, "Time to drink up."

Outside, Einstein was sniffing at the lamppost on the corner.

Leaving The King's Arms, Brett whispered, "Let's just walk straight past him in case any locals are watching us from the pub. Don't show an interest in him. With any luck, he'll follow anyway. Head across the bridge. We'll use the path on the other side of the river."

Einstein's tail began to wag. When Clare and Brett lined up at the kerb, ready to cross Langsett Road, the retriever joined them. The officers looked left and right, ignoring the dog. They strolled along Station Road until they were out of view of the pub and then turned on to the footpath beside the River Don. It was ideal, screened from the town by trees.

When they had gone far enough to be hidden from the road, Brett stopped, squatted and called softly, "Einstein! Come here." He put out his hand.

Einstein trotted up to him eagerly. Being stroked wasn't as good as getting food but the dog enjoyed the attention anyway.

Brett turned Einstein's collar to expose the name tag. Extracting the small bug from his pocket, Brett clipped it on to the same ring. Making sure that it didn't bang against the metal disc, he rotated the collar back to its original position, out of sight under Einstein's hairy chin.

Standing up beside the dog, Brett said, "It's Monday the fourth of August." He looked at his watch. "Eight-forty. Pleasant evening and the dog's caught a bug. Now, we're going back to the car. I'll give you a call on the mobile."

Clare grinned. "First sign of madness: cracked cop phones dog."

Brett offered Einstein a couple of chocolate drops which he snaffled eagerly, leaving a big slobbery patch on Brett's hand. Brett wiped away the wetness and, tailed by the retriever, headed back to the car. At the shops, Brett ignored Einstein but closed the car door carefully without crashing it into the inquisitive dog's nose. "Drive off," he said to Clare. As soon as they had put a little distance between themselves and The King's Arms, Brett called Adam. "Well? Did you pick it up? Is the game on?"

"I agree with your sensible, lovely partner,"

Adam's voice declared. "You're one cracked cop."

"Just edit a tape for me after forty-eight hours' surveillance," Brett responded. "I want to hear all the comprehensible bits."

"That won't take much tape."

Brett ignored the sceptical tone. "Just do it, Adam."

Brett looked over Liz's shoulder at her monitor and saw the start of a report on the Sergeant at Crown Court who was under suspicion of selling the details of jury members to defendants about to go to trial. "What's this? Luke Kellaway?"

"Big John's orders," Liz said. "He asked me to check it over. Someone's set fire to Kellaway's house and the chief wanted to know if there was anything in common with our overcooked cottage."

"And?"

"Nothing like it. This," Liz said, pointing to the screen, "is much more ... traditional. A grudge of some sort. Petrol poured through his letter box. Lots of damage to the door and hall. Smoke everywhere. Unpleasant but not in the same league as our case. No body bits. Seems his tennis court's been splattered with red paint as well. Vandalism or vendetta, I suppose, but it's tricky to decide if his serves are in or out now."

Brett chipped in, "Crown Court, tennis court, equally messy."

"Who was behind it?" asked Clare out of curiosity.

"Don't know," Liz answered. "But they'll be in for questioning pretty soon. I'm told they made a mistake. Used a new and unusual paint. The team on the job'll track down everyone buying it in a matter of hours."

"We *do* have our own case to work on," Brett remarked, "when you've got the time."

"Like, tomorrow morning?" said Liz.

Clare looked at her watch. "It *is* getting on. I'm supposed to be meeting a chap from the karate club."

"With an arm like yours?"

"It's not a practice or fight," Clare replied. She didn't explain further.

Brett hesitated and a wounded look flashed across his face. Then he said, "OK. You've persuaded me. Tomorrow it is."

Few would have noticed Brett's faint and fleeting expression but Clare did. He had guessed that she was involved in some intrigue and was disappointed that she had not confided in him. But she could not share everything with her partner, no matter how much she respected him.

The extra trawls of Oughtibridge, the roads around the reservoir, and the boat clubs yielded as much information as previous trawls. The extra interview with Calum Laidlow was a waste of time. Everyone remained tight-lipped, either because they knew nothing or because they were part of a conspiracy of silence. And when the DNA results arrived, they were a surprise to everyone but Clare.

"Nothing but Woodman's DNA on the body," Liz read from the report. "The killer didn't leave us a sample or the water washed it away. No way to him down that particular road. Dead end. And there's something funny about the DNA from Nathan Shaw's envelope gum and the back of the licked stamp. It isn't Woodman's, but there *is* a match."

"Oh?" Brett responded eagerly.

"Don't tell me," Clare interjected. "It matches Nathan's own sample from the chewing gum."

"In one," Liz said, impressed with Clare's deduction.

Brett looked puzzled.

In a sombre voice, Clare explained, "He's a damaged individual, is our Nathan. Very. I thought he'd probably sent the letters and toys to himself. It's his method of crying out for the attention and help that he needs," she said. "But it's a case for social services and a good psychologist, not us. I'll get on the phone and tell them."

Brett nodded. "Thanks." To himself, he said, "We're no further forward. It's all down to Einstein now."

Adam waved a cassette in the air and declared, "I hope you're not putting all your eggs in one basket. There's not much here. Nothing that's going to hatch into a sitting duck of a suspect." He slipped the tape into the machine and, before he turned it on, he explained, "I took any worthwhile chunks of chatting and edited them on to one tape, one after the other. If any of them turn out to be interesting, I'll get a transcript made, the exact time of the day it was said, and more analysis of the sound. But I doubt if it's worth it."

When he thought that no one was watching, Brett popped a small pill into his mouth. Then he sat forward and focused on the snippets of recorded conversation. Clare and Liz also listened intently.

Agitated voice of middle-aged man. *"If he'd kept to the first plan…"* Sound of a passing lorry and the hiss of air brakes. *"That damned dog! One day he'll get himself – or someone else – killed. Anyway, we wouldn't be having all this if he'd stuck with it."* Fade of voice. Response from female. *"I wish I'd never…"* Remainder inaudible.

Voice of elderly woman. *"Shoo, shoo! You can't come in here!"* Deafening barks.

Young male voice. *"Two parents! Poor thing. Must be awful. I still don't know how you manage. The rest of us can hardly cope with one."* Reply, possibly Deborah Pillinger. *"Just that they've been on edge since those cops…"* Words obscured by loud female whisper. *"There you are. Good boy, Einstein!"* Second voice again *"… got me to go back."* Another boy's voice. *"He's like everyone else. Got a thing about hacksaws at the moment. Don't know why. The cops ask a question and all of a sudden everyone's…"* Speech lost in scratching noise.

"It's a bit rich, being accused of breaking the law by someone called Lawless." Hesitation in man's voice then sober continuation. *"Seeing how the law lets us down, perhaps it's right he's called Lawless."*

Adam announced hastily, "I only left that one in to amuse you, Brett."

"Hilarious," Brett murmured, trying to concentrate on the tape.

Male voice. *"...know why the bricks didn't work."* A second man's voice. *"Nor me."* Loud shout. *"Fetch it!"* Thundering noise. Dog running and panting. Motor in background.

Joking female voice. *"...and the vicar said, "No. It's a banana!""* Raucous laughter. Male voice. *"Seriously, though, do you think Rev Hughes...?"* Interruption by middle-aged woman. *"Not a chance."*

Boisterous male voice. *"If your kid comes near mine again, there'll be hell to pay."* Slight pause. *"Get out of here, hound! Bloody nuisance."* Much quieter addition. *"And your kid's just as bad, pal. Any more bother and another one'll be dredged up at Damflask."*

"And after that," Adam announced as if his scepticism had been right all along, "the bug came adrift and stopped working. Judging by the last sound it picked up, it was probably run over."

Ignoring Adam's righteous comment, Brett exclaimed, "You said there wasn't much here. Wrong! You missed something." Immediately, he called for a replay of the short section that mentioned bricks.

Clare nodded. It was a long shot but the men might have been talking about the weights that had been placed in the sack and anchored Grayson's body in the reservoir. They might have been expressing surprise, and annoyance, that they had been dislodged and allowed the bloated body to float to the surface, buoyed by the gas of decomposition. Clare knew why Brett was so excited. She knew why he would send divers to Damflask Reservoir. If they found some new loose bricks at the bottom, the brief conversation would be enormously significant. The two men on the cassette knew something that the police didn't: there had been no evidence of the contents of the sack. That meant the men were familiar with the details of the disposal of the body. Either they had heard about it on the grapevine or they were involved in it. And on top of that, the type of brick might reveal a source. It was a good lead – as long as the snatch of conversation really was about bricks failing to keep Grayson's body submerged by coming out of the victim's sack.

Once he had listened again, Brett asked, "What's the motor? An engine?"

Adam shrugged. "Difficult to say. A tractor? Probably a bit too much of a whine for that. But they must have been in the open to throw a stick or whatever for the dog."

"OK," Brett replied thoughtfully. "Get your sound people to identify it if they can. I bet the first chap said, 'I don't know why the bricks didn't work.' If he did…" To Adam, he declared, "I want all the information phonetics can get on the two men. And Liz, I want—"

"On it, boss," she responded while tapping out an e-mail message on her keyboard. "You want flippers and snorkels."

"Let me hear the hacksaw bit again," Clare requested. "It'd be interesting if that's Deborah Pillinger, Brett."

"True, but not as interesting as the bricks. We've asked so many people about a hacksaw, it's bound to get them thinking – and talking. No one's mentioned bricks before."

"I know," Clare replied, "but the girl said, 'Got me to go back.' Someone might have got her to go back to the cottage. Maybe when we saw her there. So, who sent her back and why? Was it something to do with the hacksaw?"

"Good point," Brett agreed. Together they listened to the excerpt again then Brett said, "If someone sent her back, it sounds like it was a 'he'. *He's* like everyone else – curious about hacksaws. Adam, get your phonetics people to talk to Deborah Pillinger, Joshua Redgrave and Chelsea Magnall. Get them to work out if they're the ones on the tape. They might be. Redgrave and Magnall come from single-parent families, Deborah Pillinger doesn't."

"This hacksaw," Clare put in, "it's told us nothing. Too damaged. But maybe someone thought it was incriminating enough to try and retrieve it. You wonder who's got enough of a hold on Deborah – if it *was* her – to send her back to the scene of a crime. Her father? Boyfriend? Reverend Hughes?"

Brett was nodding. He turned towards the computer and said, "Liz…"

"Yes," she replied wearily, faking fatigue. "I'm calling it up. The report on the hacksaw."

The forensic examination had revealed nothing of importance. The saw was blackened and distorted by the full force of the fire. The blade had snapped because it had been weakened and the frame had expanded to a greater degree, stressing the blade. There was no trace of a manufacturer's mark. Any organic substances like blood or fingerprints had been evaporated or decomposed by the intense heat. There was no need for the person who had used the hacksaw to fear this sorry piece of evidence.

At Brett's shoulder, Clare said, "So much for forensic science." There was a hint of amusement in her tone. "We need to speak to Deborah Pillinger. We need to talk to Rev Hughes as well. And what about Einstein's first bit of eavesdropping? 'If he'd kept to the first plan … we wouldn't be having all this if he'd stuck with it.' Reply, 'I wish I'd never…' *If* they're talking about Tom Grayson, there was a first plan but someone didn't keep to it."

Brett broke in excitedly, saying, "You know, that makes sense. Plan A: hang him. Maybe make it look like suicide. Then 'he' worried that we'd find out. He'd be right to worry. He'd never fool Tony Rudd with a mock suicide. Then Plan B: burn the evidence. Or at least try to. That's when it all went pear-shaped. Blood everywhere and he couldn't even destroy the hands and feet easily. So, set fire to the cottage, wrap up the rest of the body and put it in the back of a van or whatever. Pick up the sack, more cord and bricks – all stuff he could get from a hardware shop – and whisk the body off to the reservoir to dump it in the early hours."

"Busy nightshift," Liz remarked.

"I wonder if the 'he' is the same as the 'he' in Deborah Pillinger's conversation," Brett mused.

Adam applied the brakes to Brett's runaway logic and imagination. "You don't know if it *was* the Pillinger girl speaking on the tape or even if the first chat was about your case. They could've been discussing tactics in a local cricket match – one that they lost because they changed their game plan. *I wish I'd never put Smith in as opener*."

"I'm well aware of that," Brett retorted, "but we need a theory to shoot at, to test. And", he urged, "we'll get on quicker the sooner you get that extra analysis underway. Times, voice and engine identification."

"By the way," Liz called just before Clare and Brett disappeared out of the door, "I guess you're not very interested right now but Luke Kellaway's vandals were hired thugs. And who hired them? I hear the trail's leading back to one of those defendants, found innocent. Weird."

Like Liz, Brett was surprised. "But Kellaway helped him get away with fraud. So why has he turned on Kellaway now? Oh, well. It's got nothing to do with us," he declared. "We haven't got time to worry about someone else's case as well as our own."

For a while Clare and Brett watched the painfully slow progress of the underwater search unit on Damflask Reservoir. Four divers were making their way from the western end towards the dam wall where a trickle of water fed River Loxley. On the surface of the reservoir, a supervisor directed the early stages of the search from a boat. Another stood beside Clare and Brett on the bank. "They're more used to hunting for disposed weapons or bodies," he commented, "but they've found a couple of bricks already. I don't think you'll be interested, though. They're old. Been underwater for ages by the look of them. There'll be plenty of others, no doubt." He was not optimistic.

Brett responded, "I'm sure you're right. But keep them all. Mine'll be newly dunked. Forensics will be able to tell the difference."

The supervisor shrugged. "Up to you," he muttered.

In Oughtibridge, Einstein strolled out of Church Close and, tail wagging enthusiastically, walked up to Brett. "Sorry," Brett said, patting him, "no treats today."

"After all he's done for you!" Clare quipped.

Brett smiled. "True. It *is* a bit mean. But thanks, Einstein. You did your job pretty well." In congratulation, he slapped the dog fondly on its flank. "Over to us now."

Clare and Brett agreed that they had to go along with Jeff Pillinger's demand that they should interview Deborah only in his presence. They found her in the roadside café with a group of five friends so they escorted her across the street and into her father's DIY store. Jeff glanced at them mistrustfully while he finished with a customer who was buying wallpaper paste and sticky tape. As soon as the door closed behind the woman, he barked, "What do you want?"

"A word with your daughter," Brett announced, "with you in attendance."

"Two of your people took a tape recording of her voice. What was that all about?" he demanded to know.

Brett waved his hand as if to dismiss a trivial matter. "Routine. Checking Debs' voice against a 999 call we took. We didn't expect to find a match and we didn't." Brett certainly did not want to reveal his unorthodox method of listening to village conversations.

Before Jeff Pillinger could ask a follow-up question, Clare began, "We'd like to ask you again, Debs, why you went up to the cottage after the fire."

"I told you," she snapped.

"Do you want to change your answer?"

"Why should I?"

Clare shrugged. "In case it was wrong. Maybe you were persuaded to go – by someone who wanted to find out what was happening up there."

"No," she mumbled.

Clare did not pursue the angle immediately. She had learned already that the voice on the cassette belonged to Debs – it had been confirmed by phonetics – so now she was probably lying. Clare noticed that Jeff Pillinger did not flinch at all during the exchange. Perhaps he was not the one who had ordered Debs back to the torched house. Or perhaps he was and yet his stony expression hid any discomfort with Clare's line of inquiry. If so, he had complete confidence that his daughter could field Clare's questions without incriminating him.

Clare tried a different tack. "Before, you said only lads went to the cottage. Do you want to tell us something different now we've talked to quite a few other people about it?" She knew that Debs would change her answer. Her friends must have told her that it had become common knowledge that she and Chelsea had gone to the derelict den.

"I meant, it's the boys' place. Sometimes – not much – they get girls to go. Me and Chelsea. That's all."

"So, you *can* change your mind. Do you want to give me a different version of your visit to the cottage after the fire? It's not a good idea to obstruct our investigation, Deborah. It's an offence. It can get you into deep waters."

"No, I don't."

Someone had a strong hold on her or the tape had misled them. Clare changed direction. "Where were you on the night the cottage burned down?

Was that one of the nights you went there with the boys?"

"No, it wasn't." As if she'd rehearsed an answer after consulting her boyfriend, she added, "I watched a horror film at home on the box."

Her answer was conveniently consistent with Joshua Redgrave's account of his activities on the evening of 24th July. "What was it called, this film?"

Jeff Pillinger butted in, asking, "What are you accusing her of?"

"Nothing at all. We're just checking where everyone was that night. I'm giving Debs a chance to show she was nowhere near the fire." Clare turned back to Deborah and said, "Well?"

" 'Night of Death'," she muttered.

Clare smiled. "Very apt. Which channel?"

"Yorkshire. And, before you ask, no, I can't remember who was in it. No big stars and they all got bumped off anyway."

"Did you see Josh at all that night?"

"No," Debs stated flatly.

"And what about you?" Clare said, looking at Deborah's father. Provocatively, she asked, "Did you take part in a night of death?"

Jeff did not change his scowling expression. Gruffly, he replied, "If you mean, did I watch the film, the answer's no. I was with my wife in The King's Arms."

"And after it closed?"

"Carl shuts up shop pretty late. When we came

back, we didn't fancy the rest of the film. We went to bed. That's it."

Clare did not see much point in struggling to move immovable objects. She likened her probing to the search for an exit from a completely blackened room. She was feeling her way slowly around the walls. Pushing against a brick wall was not likely to get her out. First, she needed to find a door. Then, some pushing and pulling would be worthwhile. Unlike the walls, a door might yield to her pressure. But the Pillingers were not a door out of the dark room.

Clare knew that her partner's natural instinct would be to find the light switch, to use evidence to illuminate the problem, rather than to fumble in the dark. But in this case much of the evidence had been destroyed by fire or water. Brett would have to put up with Clare's conventional interrogations, seeking a weak spot that she could exploit.

Of course, she didn't mention bricks to the Pillingers. She had no intention of mentioning them to any suspects. If bricks had been used to weight down the body, she did not want their significance to become apparent. That way, if anyone let slip an awareness of the use of bricks, she would know automatically that they were implicated in the crime. And that was not the only information that she and Brett had kept hidden. For the same reason they had never revealed the nature of Grayson's crimes, the likelihood that he had been hanged in the cottage, and the gruesome removal and incineration of his hands and feet. Clare hoped that these concealed details would be traps for a knowing suspect.

While he walked with Clare along Poplar Close, Brett called Liz and asked her to check the Yorkshire TV schedule for Thursday 24th July. Then he stripped down to his shirt and rolled up his sleeves, exposing two impressive tanned arms. On his right forearm, there was a line of small blue bumps.

Clare nodded towards the marks and said, "Are you coming out in sympathy with my gash?"

Brett grinned and replied, "Something like that."

"What is it? I'm not going to catch something horrible from you, am I?"

"No," Brett answered with a smile. "If I tell, you'll laugh."

"I won't," she retorted. "Well, yes, I might. It depends. Hang on! You haven't caught something from your tropical fish, have you?" she exclaimed.

"Close enough," Brett admitted. "My doctor calls it fish tank granuloma. Diagnosed last night."

Clare laughed.

Feigning an admonishing expression, Brett explained, "Seems it's an infection from bacteria in the aquarium: *Mycobacterium marinum*. Quite rare but you can get it when cleaning out the tank. It gets into the body through a cut."

"Yuck! I suppose at your grand old age you're prone to all sorts of disease. Are you marked for life?"

Brett chuckled. "No." He tapped his trouser pocket and there was the characteristic rattle of a pill bottle. "Rifampicin, an antibiotic, will clear it up."

"Ah, what you go through for those fish! I hope they appreciate it."

They arrived at the Magnalls' house and Clare reached out to ring the bell, saying, "Leave it to me, you poor decrepit thing. We don't want to make your health worse by straining your finger."

Laura Magnall came to the door and her face fell at the sight of the two detectives.

"Is Chelsea in?" asked Clare. "We need to have another word with her." Of course, Clare knew perfectly well that Chelsea was in the café down the road. That suited her purposes.

Laura glanced up and down the close as if she were ashamed to have police officers on her doorstep. "You'd better come in," she said, standing to one side. "But Chelsea hasn't done anything, you know. She's not that sort of girl."

Clare did not need to be persuaded. Chelsea was too innocent to get involved in murder. But Clare would not admit it to Laura Magnall. Quite the opposite. She wanted to apply pressure to Laura by suggesting that her daughter was under suspicion. Then, if Laura knew anything about the murder of Tom Grayson, she might spill the beans to clear her own daughter.

In the living room, Laura said, "She's out with friends at the moment. Not sure when she'll be back."

Clare hoped that it wouldn't be for at least another ten minutes. She said, "I'm afraid I have to tell you that we've got a lot of evidence that implicates Chelsea—"

"But you can't have!"

"I'm sorry," said Clare.

"What is this evidence?"

"I'm not at liberty to tell you that, but we do have to discuss it with Chelsea," Clare replied. "We need to take her to the station."

Alarmed, Laura cried, "You're not arresting her, are you?"

"Not at this stage, no. But, if you don't have a lawyer, now would be a good time." Clare didn't enjoy rubbing it in but she was determined to force Laura to reveal everything that she knew. "Look," Clare continued, "we'll go off and see another couple of people and call back later. We'll question Chelsea then."

Once a fearful Laura Magnall had closed the door on them, Brett whispered in his partner's ear, "Bully!"

"Well, sometimes it's necessary," Clare replied. "Let's sit in the car at the end of the street and see if anything happens."

"What do you expect to happen?" Brett enquired.

Clare shrugged. "I've given her time to stew, stirred things up a bit. Who knows what she might do? But it'll be interesting."

For ten minutes, nothing happened. And then Laura Magnall's green Nissan came towards them. Both Clare and Brett ducked down out of sight. Once the Nissan had accelerated away, down Church Street, Clare started the engine. Brett nodded at her and radioed for back-up. He was desperate to keep tabs on Chelsea's mother. He dictated the details of her car and reported, "Heading into Sheffield along Langsett Road, becoming Middlewood Road. We're several cars behind her and if the traffic gets bad, we'll lose her. So, we need more cars. No approach, though. Just tail her till she gets wherever she's going."

Clare glanced sideways at her partner and said with a wry smile, "Control prefers a couple of days' notice for this sort of thing."

Brett strained ahead to see Laura Magnall's car. She'd just cleared the junction before the traffic lights turned red. "Come on, come on!" he urged, as if the power of positive thinking could convert red into green.

When the traffic lights changed, Clare pulled out and streaked past the three cars ahead of her. The driver at the front, jealous of her nifty acceleration, sounded his horn at her. "Formula One here I come," she said with a grin.

Brett informed Control, "Coming up to Hillsborough and Penistone Road. The Nissan's even further in front of us now but I can just see it. Hang on. She's turned left, away from the city centre."

At the junction, Clare tore up the inside lane and also turned left, trying to catch up a little.

Going over the river, Brett reported, "She's gone right on to Herries Road, heading east into Shirecliffe. Have we got any back-up yet?"

"Two unmarked cars on their way. One coming down Barnsley Road from the north. Should intercept near the hospital. Another's coming from the centre, currently stuck in Penistone Road traffic."

"Great," Brett murmured. He jolted forward as Clare slammed on the brakes and joined a line of stationary cars.

Waiting in the queue for a roundabout, Clare grumbled, "Call this a car chase? I should've burnt half our rubber on to the road by now. It's not like this in the movies. In Sheffield, it's slow motion." She tapped the steering wheel with itchy fingers.

"We'd do better on push-bikes," Brett remarked.

It wasn't an exaggeration. On cue, an old man wobbled past on his bike on the inside, almost scraping their car.

"You could jump out and commandeer his bike," Clare joked, "but you might have trouble keeping up if she goes to junction 34 and on to the M1."

While Clare inched her way round the traffic island, Brett kept up his running commentary, notifying Control, "Coming up to the Northern General soon." To Clare he added, "At this pace, we'll be able to pop into the hospital and both have check-ups on our arms." Then peering ahead, he cried, "She's turning left just after Barnsley Road. It looks like Firth Park, Grimesthorpe or Wincobank. And this," Brett groaned, "is where we lose her. We're stuck in a jam and she's off up Firth Park Road. Tell me you've got that car in the area, Control."

A smug voice replied, "Yes, we have. Cavalry to the rescue. They've picked her up. Will report back."

Brett sat back in the seat and let out a long breath. "Phew."

Clare cruised towards Wincobank, following the instructions on the latest position of the other police car. Eventually, Control announced, "The Nissan's stopped. Wincobank shops. Your target's gone into a butchers – with the awful name, Joint of Meat. Must be after her Sunday roast."

As she set off towards the shops, Clare said, "Do you reckon we're about to see Jamie Lennox at work?"

"Sure do. You know, the pathologist at the cottage suggested we start with the local butcher."

Once Clare had parked within sight of both the Nissan and the shop, Brett nodded towards the butcher's and remarked, "I wish we'd got Einstein plus bug in there."

"Einstein would love it as well. Different reason, though." Dabbing sun screen on her nose, cheeks and forehead, Clare said, "Well, are we going to join the party?" She pointed at the Joint of Meat.

"What do you think – as we're doing this your way?"

"I say no. I like to tackle them one at a time. It means we can check for inconsistencies. It means one never knows what the other's said to us. Makes them uncomfortable. Together, there's strength in numbers. You don't want them feeling strong."

"OK," Brett agreed. By radio, he arranged for the other police car to follow Laura Magnall when she left the shop. He wanted to know if she was going straight back home or whether she had other visits in mind.

Two minutes after Chelsea's mum had emerged from the butcher's, Clare and Brett got out and crossed the road. Inside the shop, they hardly recognized Jamie Lennox. He was disguised in an apron and hat, he was brandishing a large knife, almost a hatchet, poised over a leg of mutton. When he saw who had come in, he looked round nervously. He was probably wondering if the police officers had noticed Laura, asking himself if their arrival so soon after Laura's departure was coincidence or design.

"Sorry to bother you at work," Brett began, "but one or two things have cropped up."

"Oh?" Jamie responded, still clutching the cleaver. Perhaps he was hoping that the interruption to his work would be brief.

"We were thinking about your rowing boat. Do you allow anyone else to use it regularly? Do you have an arrangement with anyone?"

"No, not really."

"Not really?"

"If you still think it was used to … do what you say, it wasn't with my permission," Jamie claimed.

Brett tried to keep Jamie guessing for a while longer about the real reason for their visit by asking about something else first. "You told us last time that Einstein, the retriever, was often around your place in Oughtibridge. Did you ever take scraps back for him?"

Finally Jamie put down the knife, realizing that the police officers had more business with him than he had bargained for. He propped himself against the work surface and said, "No. But I suppose I go home smelling of meat. It must attract him."

Clare said, "Do you know Jeff Pillinger?"

Jamie nodded. "The hardware store. I don't mix with him socially – not my idea of fun - but I know him, yes."

"What *is* Pillinger's idea of fun?" Brett queried.

"Oh, it's not just him. A lot of the life of the village

is centred on The King's Arms. The heart of the village. I don't drink."

"Do you know Laura Magnall?" Clare asked bluntly.

Jamie paused. "Laura Magnall?"

"Yes. Lives in Poplar Close. Her daughter's friendly with Deborah Pillinger." Clare could tell that Jamie was deciding if he dared to risk lying. But he knew that he would put himself in a difficult position if he denied knowing Laura when two police officers might have witnessed her calling on him: once here in his shop and once at home.

"Why do you want to know?"

"We're trying to get a feel for all the relationships in the town – and we're interviewing anyone who knows Chelsea Magnall." There was no harm in reinforcing the pressure on Chelsea, Clare believed.

"Yes. I know Laura and Chelsea. And I can't imagine Chelsea getting up to—"

Interrupting, Clare asked, "How would you describe your relationship with Laura?"

"She's… We go out with each other."

"With Chelsea's approval?"

"I think so."

"You think of her as a daughter?" Clare asked.

"That would be … premature," Jamie answered.

"But you'd protect her if she was in a spot of bother?"

Jamie hesitated and then replied, "Not if I thought she was in the wrong."

"All right," Clare said in a tone that suggested she was getting down to business. "Has she ever used your rowing boat, Mr Lennox?"

"No, not..." Jamie faltered and admitted, "Not much but, yes, she's been in it."

"So she's familiar with it. Interesting," Clare murmured deliberately as if she were thinking aloud. "What did you just talk to Laura about? Chelsea?"

The butcher breathed deeply and nodded. "There's no point denying it: Laura's worried. Of course she's worried. She thinks you're ... hounding her daughter for no reason. Chelsea's done nothing. Nothing that normal teenagers don't get up to. And a lot less than most do."

"So, what did Laura say?"

Jamie wiped his hands on his apron to give himself a little time to think. "She just needed a bit of comfort and reassurance really."

Clare examined his face closely and then said, "Maybe, but that's not all. What did you talk about?"

"Look," Jamie muttered, "if you want to know you should ask Laura. I think she may... Anyway, I encouraged her to ... just be honest with you. Chelsea's got nothing to hide."

Clare's brow creased. "You mean you or Laura *have* got something to hide?"

Jamie was feeling increasingly uncomfortable. "I didn't say that."

The butcher sighed with relief when a customer

came in. For a few moments, Lennox could serve sausages and bacon, untroubled by awkward questions. The customer glanced furtively at the waiting detectives as if they were robbers and said, "Are you all right, Mr Lennox?"

Jamie managed a smile. "It's OK. They're ... friends." He did not want to admit to a valued customer that he was tangling with the police. She might look for a more reputable butcher.

Clare was keen to interview Laura Magnall, especially if her boyfriend had just persuaded her to speak out, but she also felt that she was softening Jamie Lennox. Now she'd got her fangs into him, she did not want to let go. As soon as the woman had left the Joint of Meat with her provisions, Clare continued, "If Chelsea's as innocent as you say, don't you owe it to her to tell us what you know? Perhaps it'll put her in the clear."

Brett retreated into a corner of the shop to answer his mobile phone.

Jamie watched Brett out of the corner of his eye while he said to Clare, "I don't know anything." There was exasperation in his tone.

Clare leaned on the counter and retorted, "I don't believe that for a moment. You know plenty."

Jamie shrugged helplessly.

"Does Chelsea go camping – with one of those tents carried in a canvas bag?" asked Clare, trying to unsettle him with different twists and turns.

Surprised and perplexed, Jamie answered, "I

think she's been camping, yes, but I don't know anything about her tent."

"What do you think of Reverend Hughes?"

"What is this?" Jamie spluttered, bamboozled by Clare's unpredictable inquiry. "He's … I don't know … an ordinary vicar."

"Fire and brimstone or forgive and forget?"

Suddenly realizing why the detective had posed the question, Jamie said, "He preaches forgiveness." The butcher paused before adding significantly, "A good message as far as I'm concerned."

Clare was in two minds. She believed that there was a passage to the truth by pressurizing Laura Magnall through a daughter who was vulnerable to accusations, but she also wanted to squeeze Lennox. Having indicated that Chelsea was a key suspect, though, she could not easily shift her position and implicate Jamie Lennox. He would know that she was fishing around, making empty threats. In an instant, though, she concocted a way forward. "You know what I think?" she said to the butcher. "I think you know perfectly well what happened at the cottage and down by the reservoir. The only question is: how? Because Chelsea was involved and she's said something, because Laura Magnall told you something, or because you were in the thick of it. Chelsea couldn't have acted on her own."

"But—"

"What size shoes do you wear?"

"I … er … size ten."

Clare nodded knowingly. She was thinking of the evidence for a scuffle outside the cottage. "In that case we'll be sending someone round to you to take a look at every pair you've got."

Brett rejoined the fray and asked, "Mr Lennox. Could you tell me the nature of your conversation with Reverend Hughes on the morning of Friday 25th July?"

16

Jamie Lennox clutched the edge of the work surface. For a moment he was startled and dumbfounded. "Reverend Hughes?" he gasped. "How did you know…?"

"It doesn't matter," Brett responded. "I'd just like to know what you talked about. That's all. He called it a counselling session. So, what were you counselled about?"

"It was a private matter."

"Not good enough," Brett said abruptly.

"Oh, I see," Jamie murmured. "Your people have spoken to Rev Hughes and he mentioned our … chat, but he wouldn't say what it was about because it *was* private."

"So I'm asking you," Brett said.

"Well," Jamie replied, composing himself, "it's a

bit embarrassing. I hope you won't mention this to Laura but we talked about whether he'd be willing to marry us. If the time came."

Clare and Brett stared at him and briefly at each other. Brett declared incredulously, "And Reverend Hughes thought that was so important to our investigation he'd phone our incident room about it?"

Jamie shrugged. "Apparently." He picked up the shiny hatchet again. "Perhaps he thought you ought to know that Laura and I are … a couple. Perhaps he saw some significance in our relationship that … escapes me. And you, it seems."

Clare decided to intervene. "OK," she put in, "that's your explanation – for now. We're going to see Chelsea. If you want to help a girl who, it seems, could become your stepdaughter, you'd better think again and give us a call." She deposited a card on the serving counter. With Brett she strode out of the Joint of Meat.

Back in the car, Brett asked, "What do you think? Is he our butcher? And did Laura dash over here to warn him? Warn him that she'd have to defend her daughter by coming clean and pointing the finger at him."

"I don't know," Clare answered, "but he's hiding something." She told her partner about the shoes and immediately Brett contacted Forensics to organize a comparison of every pair of Lennox's shoes with one of the impressions near the cottage.

Then he said to Clare, "In that phone call I also got a bulletin on Laura Magnall. She's not gone home yet. She's called in at The King's Arms."

"Thirsty work, tangling with the ace cop team: Lawless and Tilley."

"Let's follow her trail," Brett decided. "We'll try our luck in the pub after she's left it."

Clare glanced over her shoulder and then accelerated away from the kerb. "And what about that horror film? Any news?"

"It checks out, according to Liz. Late night B-movie on Yorkshire. No big names, just lots of blood and gore. Either Debs and Josh watched it or they've done their research."

By the time that Clare parked in the pub's car park, Control had informed them that Laura had arrived at home. "OK. Let's go in and see if she's opened a can of worms."

In the late afternoon, there was hardly anybody in the bar but Jeff Pillinger was supping a pint of beer, huddled with Greenacre at the bar. When the police officers came in, Jeff grimaced and Carl smiled broadly. "Welcome!" the landlord said rather too cheerfully. "What can I get for you?"

"Nothing, thanks," Brett replied politely.

"On duty again?" Carl asked.

"Always," Brett responded. "But you're not, apparently," he said to Pillinger.

"Closed Wednesday afternoons," the storekeeper explained. "To make up for being open all day

Saturday – as you know. You've called on me at work the last two Saturdays," he said resentfully. "Anyway, if a local's desperate for a nail, they know where to find me."

Looking at Jeff Pillinger, Clare said, "You'll know Chelsea, no doubt. One of your Deborah's friends."

Jeff nodded. "Nice girl."

Carl butted in. "You told me you were getting on well with your case, maybe close to an arrest. Surely you can't mean Chelsea! You must be joking. She's just a kid."

Eager to protect his daughter's best friend, Jeff added, "For one thing, Debs said Chelsea called in at my place late on the night the cottage went up. She can't be the one."

"Who is then?"

Both men shrugged. "Don't know."

Clare's tactic was working. She was amused by the men's enthusiasm to protect an innocent girl like Chelsea. Clare decided to play it rough to see if she could force them not just to deny Chelsea's involvement but to implicate whoever they were sheltering. "You two may not know who's behind it but who did Laura accuse? She called in a little while ago. That's why you know we're interested in Chelsea. Her mother told you."

Carl and Jeff looked uneasy. The landlord took the lead. He said, "Well … Laura's in a difficult position. You've put the frighteners on her and she's … frightened. Split loyalties."

Clare smelled victory. "Split loyalties between Chelsea and…?"

Carl Greenacre passed his hand over his shiny head – perhaps a memory of running his fingers through his hair – and answered reluctantly, "I don't think you need to bother Laura again. I think we'd better…" He nudged Jeff and said, "Go on."

Jeff took a deep breath. "I don't like to…" He paused before muttering, "I don't know if this is relevant but I've been thinking. You were asking about hacksaws. I checked back on some of my sales." He took a swig of beer as if to give himself strength to reveal a damning fact. "A week last Friday I sold a hacksaw to Mr Lennox at the top of the hill. Something about a replacement for a broken one."

Clare grinned widely. "Thank you, Mr Pillinger. That's helpful. Very helpful. We don't need to trouble you again for a while." The pressure on Chelsea Magnall was paying dividends. Clare believed the door to her darkened room was beginning to yield.

Outside the pub, she whispered to Brett, "Helpful *and* precisely what I expected."

"It was?" Brett queried.

She nodded. "Strange that a day after Pillinger sold that saw – on the Saturday when we spoke to him – he couldn't remember who'd bought it but he does now. We *have* stirred up a hornet's nest, haven't we?"

"You're enjoying this, aren't you?"

"Mmm." She got into the car and said, "They

seemed keen for us not to disturb Laura again, didn't they?"

Brett smiled. "Poplar Close, it is then."

But before they reached the Magnalls' house, Brett took a call from the team at the reservoir. They had discovered a small collection of identical new bricks. "All right," Brett responded without hesitation. "We're still in the area. With you in a few minutes."

Clare would have preferred to continue with her series of interviews but she diverted to Damflask Reservoir. On the way through the narrow lanes, she said, "Pillinger may be the heavy around here but Greenacre's definitely the boss, you know, despite how daft he looks. You saw how he dictated the conversation in the pub. He's the unofficial community leader."

"Yes. He took responsibility for blaming Lennox."

Clare glanced at Brett. "Now why did they do that? Is Jamie Lennox living up to his butcher's reputation or is he just being offered to us as a scapegoat? A more palatable one than Chelsea." She brought the car to a halt by the underwater search unit's vehicles in the entrance to the rowing club.

They found the supervisor standing like a proud fisherman next to a prize catch. His divers had landed eight bricks and made a small stack of them. Brett waved away the flies and knelt by the pile. "That's probably about as many as you could get in the sack," he murmured. Looking up at the team leader, he said, "Good work."

"A chap called Neville from Forensic's on his way."

Too impatient to wait for an official report, Brett took one of the bricks and stood up with it. "Tell him I've taken one. I'm not ruining evidence because the water will have done that already. All Neville will be able to do is identify the type and maybe how long they've been underwater." He showed the trophy to Clare and commented, "See? Thinner than your normal brick and flat top and bottom." He ran a finger round the four sides and continued, "Ridges here."

"Not a building brick at all, then," Clare deduced. "What is it?"

"The type used for block paving. The lumps on the sides stop them moving against each other when they're laid down and they're flat for walking or driving on."

"Uncommon?" Clare queried hopefully.

"I don't think so," Brett answered. "Quite expensive. But I'll tell you one thing: you last saw them at Jamie Lennox's house. His drive is block paved. Perhaps he had a few spare bricks."

Clare nodded. "Perhaps. Or perhaps whoever laid his drive for him had some left over."

The supervisor interjected, "Are we done here? We haven't covered the whole reservoir but I imagine the job's over."

"Don't your divers like a nice dip on a day like

this?" Brett said cheerfully. He was always happier and more optimistic with some hefty physical evidence in his hand.

"Never mind the divers. I'm getting fed up with these damn gnats. They're eating me alive. I'm coming up in all sorts of nasty bumps."

Brett laughed. "Thanks. Call it a day. Go and get yourself some antihistamines."

Depositing the brick in the car boot, out of sight, Brett said to Clare, "Let's call in at the Lennox place before we go back to Laura Magnall."

"Yeah, I know," she murmured. "You want to get on your hands and knees – while he's not around." Inside the car, she added, "As soon as you get the smell of an exhibit that'll look good in court, you forget simple questioning." She reversed out of the track and spun round expertly in the road.

"That's not fair, Clare," Brett protested. "We'll take a quick look at Lennox's drive and then it's back to you – and the Magnalls." He watched her driving for a moment and then added, "You're working wonders on this case. I wouldn't dream of stopping you now."

At Jamie's house, making sure no one was watching, Brett placed the wet brick on top of one of the blocks making up the driveway. It was exactly the same shape and colour: mottled reddish-brown. It seemed to be identical.

"You know," Clare murmured, "we've been some-where else with this sort of paving. Where was it?"

She shut her eyes to concentrate, trying to see the place in her mind.

"You're right," Brett replied. "It was the church. Same type of blocks in a pattern with bluish-grey ones, if I remember rightly. Interesting."

With Clare, he got back into the car and they cruised down the hill to Poplar Road. They turned into it and drove along to Poplar Close at the end. Chelsea was still not at home. Clare suspected that she had been back but that her mother had found an excuse to send her away again so that she didn't have to face an interrogation. But Clare was much more interested in Laura herself. She looked worn. Clare's policy of letting her stew for a while had been successful, but Clare still detected an element of defiance in her eyes. Laura Magnall was not yet a broken woman. Clare expected to have to wind up the tension yet more and then allow Laura a further period of reflection before she'd crack.

"So where is Chelsea?" Clare began.

"I don't know. Still out, I guess. It *is* the summer holiday," Laura replied, trying to hold herself together.

"You can't go on sheltering her for ever, you know. There's a very serious charge to answer."

"Look," Laura proclaimed, using an argument that she had carefully rehearsed, "Chelsea didn't have anything to do with it. She can't have. She doesn't drive. She couldn't have taken this body you've found from the cottage to the reservoir."

Immediately, Clare pounced. "Who said any such journey happened?"

"Well… It's obvious. It must have."

"Why? It's common knowledge we found a body at the reservoir but we've never said anyone was killed at the cottage."

Laura looked out of the living room window for a second, as if gathering strength, and then stammered, "Maybe not. But … that's what the village is saying. Murder in the cottage, body thrown in Damflask."

"Then the village knows more than it's letting on – and so do you," Clare retorted.

"No, I don't know—"

"I'll tell you what we'll do," Clare said. "We'll leave you and Chelsea to think about it overnight. Sleep on it. And I think you'll decide to be a bit more open and honest with us tomorrow morning. Because it gets heavy then. Into the station. There'll be trouble for Chelsea and a charge of obstructing our investigation for you – unless you tell us what you know."

On the way back to Sheffield, Liz called. Cryptically she said, "As soon as you get back, you'll want to come and see me."

"Oh? Why? What have you got?"

"You wouldn't want me to tell you by phone. You never know who might be listening in. But while you've been charging round the countryside, chasing the wrong people, I've been solving this crime."

"All right, Liz," said Brett. "We'll be with you in twenty minutes."

"Thirty in this traffic," Clare muttered.

"I was thinking about the Kellaway affair," Liz explained, "and doing a bit of homework. Luke Kellaway's criminal chums wouldn't be fire-bombing and repainting his house without a reason. Perhaps they thought he was going to shop them and they were warning him not to – in their own sweet way. Why would he shop them, though?"

Brett chipped in, "If they knew he was under investigation for leaking jury details. They'd think he might talk and land them back in court for jury nobbling."

"Bingo!" Liz cried. "That's what I thought."

"This *is* leading to the Grayson/Woodman case, isn't it?" Brett checked.

Liz took a drink of coffee and then held up her arms, about fifty centimetres apart. "We're about that far away at the moment but in a couple of minutes we're going to be this close," she said, bringing her right thumb and forefinger almost together.

"Can't wait," Brett responded with a smile.

"It's obvious," Liz retorted. "I'd have thought a brainy chap like you... Anyway, how would those fraud defendants know we were looking into our police Sergeant at Crown Court? Someone must have told them. Who? Someone who knows about the investigation and doesn't like to see crooks running rings round the law. Someone who thinks crooks get away with it too much, too often. Know anyone like that?"

Brett was nodding slowly. "I see where you're going. Bob Baird?"

"Maybe that university education wasn't wasted on you after all."

Brett had to smile. Liz's respect for rank was negligible but her work rate and humour were prodigious. Brett could take her jibes all day long when she gave him results as well as laughs. "I can see how you're heading for our case but I don't see any evidence – only theories."

"OK. The boss orders proof – that's what he's going to get. Soon. For now, you accept that our custody sergeant could've been affected by counting in truck-loads of crooks and counting most of them back out again. So, he runs a side-line – for all the right reasons – of fixing the baddies that the law couldn't touch. He drops Luke Kellaway in it by telling Kellaway's contacts he's about to crack under investigation. Now, you want proof. I've been playing with my new toy: checking phone calls. I've got to do something when I'm stuck in the incident room all the time. Anyway, I wasn't allowed to run CaseCall on Baird's phone records because his data's protected. Apparently, as police officers, all our phone records are restricted. I had to go to the chief. He issued the authority to BT and guess what? Bob Baird called Kellaway's fraud contact two days before Kellaway's house got done over."

"All right, you might well have solved someone else's case," Brett said. "But what about ours? You're going to tell me Bob Baird must have leaked Ray Woodman's – or Tom Grayson's – past to someone in Oughtibridge. And he did it because he decided Woodman wasn't punished enough by his prison sentence. Baird let the Outibridge community know they had an abuser in their midst and some self-appointed executioner did the rest." Brett paused to think and then continued, "I see. While you were tinkering in Bob's phone details you spotted an Oughtibridge number. Baird called one of our suspects! Who was it, Liz?"

Liz laughed and put up her hands to halt his zeal. "Wrong. Much more subtle than that. I checked for Oughtibridge numbers but didn't find any. So, I delved around in Baird's record and family history. Remember? You had me check out the families of police officers for any history of abuse. Nothing. But he's got a sister: Maureen Baird. I didn't follow her up before, because I was looking for problems when she was young and she didn't have any as far as I could tell. Maureen married a few years ago. The blushing bride got hitched … you'll be fascinated to know … to someone called Carl Greenacre. Well-known resident of the Oughtibridge community."

"The unofficial leader," Clare murmured.

"Now that," Brett exclaimed, patting Liz on her shoulder, "is what I call good stuff. See? I told you you'd do us proud on the computer. Brilliant. But," he added, "I owe you one. I'll get you in on the end-play of this case. Out in the field."

"I'll believe it when I feel the sun on my face. Anyway, the answer to your next question's yes," Liz announced. "Bob Baird's on duty right now. I got the Kellaway team to organize a substitute custody sergeant – he's waiting to take over as soon as you give the go-ahead – but I claimed priority on talking to Baird because we're a murder inquiry. You're getting first crack at him. But before you go, have a look at the voice analysis on the two men Adam taped talking about bricks. Won't take long. It's as brief as my time out of the incident room."

The computerized report did not help a great deal. *Two males without pronounced accents but both native Yorkshire and possibly white. Working class, probably in their forties.* Brett groaned. "Reminds me of something Carl Greenacre said. Most of his customers are white and about forty."

"Including Pillinger," Clare noted.

"So's Lennox."

The other noises on the tape were much more helpful. The dog had almost certainly run along a stony path and the motor in the background remained unidentified but could have been a lathe.

"There's a stone entry up the side of Pillinger's shop and I bet he's got a lathe," Clare said.

"The road outside Jamie Lennox's house is hardly a road at all: a stony track. And his workshop looked quite posh. He might well have a lathe in it," Brett replied. "And there's a gravel path that leads to the garden at the back of The King's Arms."

"Greenacre's in his fifties. Too old – and I can't see him playing with Einstein," said Clare.

Brett thanked Liz and asked her to send for the relief custody sergeant while he and Clare had an unpleasant talk with Bob Baird. The idea of a corrupt police officer appalled Brett. If it was true that Bob Baird had released confidential information that allowed someone in Oughtibridge to take the law into their own hands, Brett would understand his motives but deplore his methods.

Clare set up Interview Room 2, turned on the tape machine and introduced the session with Bob Baird, giving the time, date and officers present. When she'd finished, Brett said in a chatty tone, "You've been custody sergeant for quite a while, Bob. How long's this stint been?"

"Ten months," he said warily.

"Other duties in a couple of months' time?"

"I guess so."

"It's not the easiest job, custody officer."

Bob decided not to take the bait. He answered simply, "No." Then he added, "What's this all about, Brett?"

"You once said to me that seeing crooks walk away from the cells made you mad. You talked about non-stick evidence and clever-clogs lawyers. I think you called it soul-destroying. Is that right?"

"Er … yes. That sounds like me. But—"

"How far would you go to make sure a villain gets what he deserves?"

Bob's face creased. "How do you mean?" It wasn't that he was puzzled by the question: he wasn't sure how to answer it and he was playing for time.

Brett glanced around the bare room where Sergeant Baird had placed so many of the people who had passed through his hands. "This isn't a pleasant business, Bob. Let's get it over with quickly." Formally, Brett asked, "Did you release the details of the convicted abuser, Ray Woodman – known here as Tom Grayson – to the public?"

"The public? No."

"I have to push you on this one, Bob," Brett stated in the cold atmosphere of the intimidating room. "Did you leak any information on him to *anyone*?"

"This talk about nailing crooks, you know – most of it is just talk."

"I'm sure it is," Brett responded. "But I'm

interested in the bit that's not just talk. The bit where you actually took action. Action that's … unwise for a police officer."

Bob leaned back in his chair and sighed. He looked first at Clare and then at Brett, realizing that they were both content to sit in dreadful silence and wait for him to make a statement. He came forward again and put his elbows on the desk. "I'm not the only one," he said, staring at Clare. "When I said I'd hold scum like Telfer while Sergeant Tilley hit him, I didn't mean it literally."

"Just as well," Brett responded swiftly. "And just as well that the suspect, Mr Telfer, wasn't hit by anyone. But let me bring you back to Tom Grayson. Did you say anything about him to any outsider?"

The custody sergeant's unsubtle threat to reveal Clare's outburst was not working. Inspector Lawless would shield his partner as much as he could but he was also going to pursue an answer to his question, no matter what came to the surface. Bob Baird could see the determination in his interrogator's face. He would not get out of the interview room until Brett was satisfied. Bob decided not to make life awkward for Sergeant Tilley by accusing her of malpractice. After all, he approved of her attack on a crook who deserved it. And Bob had his principles. He was a good man. That's why he had a campaign to rid the world of evil men when the judicial system failed.

"Look," Bob said, cutting into the silence, "if the courts won't put abusers away for long enough – to protect our kids – then people have to take action themselves. Who can blame them?"

"We can," Brett replied. "We have the law, so we don't need mob rule."

"Grayson got what he deserved," Bob blurted out, digging a very deep hole for himself. "I reckon someone's done us all a service by getting rid of him."

"I'm not here for a debate, Bob. I'm here to get one simple answer from you. But," Brett argued, "what if Tom Grayson had changed his ways, as well as his name, when someone got rid of him? How would that make you feel? The system didn't get the time to help him cure himself of his anti-social behaviour. Tragic for everyone concerned. Now, who did you tell?"

"My sister works with kids in the Oughtibridge area. Part-time when she's not helping at the pub," Bob said. "Maybe she'd say it's not worth the risk of having people like Woodman around. Abusers aren't often cured, you know. They re-offend."

Brett refused to be distracted again by the controversy. He kept to the point. "Did she know about Grayson?"

Bob slumped in his chair and nodded.

"For the benefit of the tape," Clare announced, "Sergeant Baird nodded."

"How?" Brett enquired curtly.

Bob exhaled heavily and admitted, "I told her. But she didn't … you know… She didn't kill him."

"When did you tell her?"

"I don't know. Three or four weeks ago."

"Thank you," Brett declared, standing up. "Interview concluded."

Clare read out the time and turned off the tape. On the way out of the room, she turned and said, "Sorry, Bob. But there's a line and you stepped over it. Now the Kellaway team'll want a word with you as well."

Brett added, "Time to make a phone call, Bob. To your lawyer. No one else."

The custody sergeant nodded miserably. He was resigned to his fate. He would lose his job over a matter of principle.

18

"Up to a point," Clare said, "Baird's right, you know."

"What point is that?" asked Brett.

"Well, he was trying to stop Luke Kellaway's nasty game and protect kids in Oughtibridge. For the right reasons, as you said, Liz. Not that *I* approve," Clare added hastily.

Brett was in philosophical mood. "If our ultimate boss – the law – fails and a bad guy gets away with something," he mused, "it's a brave and very foolish person who tries to make up for it. A recipe for injustice. Some would say only Reverend Hughes' boss has the authority and wisdom to put things right." He glanced skywards. But he saw only stars.

"What I mean is," Clare replied, "I understand Bob's anger. Even though it's been taken too far –

much too far – by someone who's got no right to pass judgement." She shook her head in sadness. "I keep hearing that social services supervisor saying he had real hope that Tom Grayson was a reformed character."

They were sitting with Liz outside in the pub garden, relishing the cool night and cold beer. The sound of raucous folk music leaked from the back door.

"There's no excuse for anyone taking the law into their own hands. Never," Brett stated.

"And it doesn't even help," Clare remarked. "It'll just drive the abusers underground – where we can't keep track of them. I'd rather have them out in the open – registered – so we can keep an eye on them, making sure they're not up to their tricks."

"If the system does fail," Brett said, "I think it's *after* conviction. It goes for punishment in a big way because it's what the people demand. But a prison sentence is normally followed by more offending, more damage to victims, more time inside. That's the problem. Sometimes, all it seems to offer is punishment and revenge instead of treatment and rehabilitation. The trouble is, any politician who favours rehabilitation over revenge is accused of being soft on crime. It's a vote loser."

"And it doesn't go down well with the great opinion-makers of our time – the tabloids," Liz added.

"True," Brett agreed, taking another drink.

"Anyway, who's first in the morning? We're spoilt for choice. Maureen and Carl Greenacre, Laura Magnall, Jamie Lennox, a visit to Forensics?"

"Well, I know what I'll be doing," Liz muttered.

"Oh?"

"The Greenacres have become the key," she replied. "They received the information about Grayson. So, where did it go after that?"

Brett nodded. "Telephone trickery again," he surmised. "To find out who the Greenacres have been talking to in the past month. Yes. Good idea. Much of the talk will have been face-to-face but, you never know, they might have gone in for quite a few phone chats as well."

"More work for iTel and CaseCall. I'll start with the Greenacres, find out who they've called a lot in the locality, and then widen the search to those contacts. Build up a network of who's calling who. Friends and family."

"More underhand stuff." Brett sighed but agreed to it. After all, by using Einstein, he had been forced to be underhand himself.

Clare said, "I want to press Laura Magnall. She'll have an uncomfortable night tonight. Ripe for picking tomorrow morning. But…"

"What?"

"I can't help thinking of Einstein. It's tenuous, I know, but he barked like crazy outside The King's Arms. You remarked on it yourself. Perhaps he knows something we don't. Perhaps he's got something against the Greenacres. Like, they took away his meal ticket, Tom Grayson."

"OK," Brett put in. "Here's what we'll do. Liz'll exercise the software—"

"Surprise, surprise!" Liz muttered.

Ignoring her, Brett continued, "We'll get someone to bring Laura *and* Chelsea Magnall in for questioning. Keep them waiting in separate rooms while we pay a visit to Forensics to get the latest, then go and talk to the Greenacres. By the time we get back, Laura should be ready to talk."

"Pressure-cooked," Clare guessed.

When they left the pub, the three of them went their separate ways. Clare drove away to see a friend from her karate club. Liz went to meet a man who, she believed, was worth dating. He seemed warm, witty and sexy. He might even tolerate the demands of her police work. She set off feeling strangely optimistic about her future. Brett decided to go back to work. He said that he wanted to look up a few things in records.

On Thursday morning Neville showed off in front of Clare. He held up a pair of soiled shoes and boasted, "Lennox tried to hide them – dump them wrapped up with kitchen waste in his dustbin – but we found them. And, yes, they match the impressions outside the cottage." Choosing his words carefully, Neville concluded, "Someone in these shoes, or in the same type of shoe, was outside the cottage at some point in the recent past. And he might have been in a scuffle of some sort."

"Thanks, Neville," Brett said. "Anything else?"

"No. Still working on the bricks."

"OK, we'll get a move on. It's going to be a busy day."

On the familiar road to Oughtibridge, Brett commented, "We've got a lot against Jamie Lennox. The fact that he's probably been to the cottage when he said he hadn't. Otherwise, he wouldn't have tried to get rid of the shoes. His profession. The rowing boat. The bricks matching his block paving. The hacksaw Pillinger said he bought. Butcher's van for transporting the body. And Reverend Hughes suggesting that I have a chat with him."

"Mmm. A good hoard of evidence, for sure," Clare admitted, "but where's the motive? And why doesn't he make a convincing murderer – even though he's a butcher?"

"You mean, *you're* not convinced."

Clare grinned and nodded.

"You're sold on Jeff Pillinger."

"You might say that. You see, I don't believe yesterday's hacksaw business. Too convenient. Laura saw Pillinger and Greenacre, had a few words, and suddenly Chelsea's got an alibi through the Pillinger family and our DIY expert recalls a damning piece of evidence against Jamie Lennox. I bet he couldn't produce a till receipt for it. As for the shoes, Lennox is scared. Of course he'd try to remove the evidence that he was up at the cottage. It doesn't mean he's our man."

"Well," Brett said, "if we don't get anywhere with the Greenacres and Laura today, we'll be chasing those things. As well as having further words with Lennox and Rev Hughes, our block paving experts."

Suddenly, Clare sat bolt upright and pointed at the windscreen with her right hand. "What on earth's that?" she cried.

"I'm not sure," Brett answered peering at the glass, "but, you know, I think it's that stuff we used to call rain – before global warming put an end to it."

Really, it was no more than a faint drizzle but at last Sheffield had been cloaked by cloud. For once sunshine failed to get through. The ground absorbed the rainfall like a thirsty sponge.

"Wonderful," Clare sighed. "What a relief."

The stones of The King's Arms car park had been parched white but now they were shiny wet and several shades darker.

Inside, Carl Greenacre was sitting at one of the tables in the lounge, bent over the accounts, and Maureen was polishing the bar. It was impractical to interview them separately, so Clare brought them together at Carl's table.

"Again?" Carl queried, still jovial and apparently unconcerned. "You're becoming permanent fixtures round here."

"Not for much longer," Clare responded with implied threat. "Mrs Greenacre," she asked, "how long has it been since you heard from your brother?"

"Bob? I don't rightly know." She shrugged. "Why?" She glanced at Carl.

"In the last month, say?"

"We don't keep in touch a lot but, in the last month, I should think so."

Clare enquired, "And what did you talk about?"

"Oh, this and that. You know, the weather, business—"

"What business?"

"The pub."

"And Bob's business?"

"I guess so. A bit."

Clare smiled. "You're being very vague, Mrs Greenacre. I suspect you talked about a very particular part of Bob's business. That's what he told us, anyway."

Maureen frowned. "Bob said…" She shook her head and looked to her husband for support.

Quickly, Clare asked Carl, "Were you in on this brother-and-sister chat?"

"Yes," he admitted. "Over a cup of coffee and jacket potato in the café, as I recall."

Clare did not like the hint of mischief in Carl Greenacre's eyes. And she wondered why he was so keen to tell her where they had met Bob. "Not a pie and a pint in here?" she queried.

"No."

"Your brother, Mrs Greenacre, is in custody at the moment, answering some tricky questions, facing a charge of perverting the course of justice and disclosing confidential information. I've heard his version of what he told you. Now," she prompted, "I'd like to hear your side of the story – before you're in custody as well. What did he tell you about his work?"

"Not a great deal," Maureen answered. She glanced across the table at Carl and saw him nod. "It just came out in the general chat. He mentioned a chap called Grayson, just moved into a place up in Poplar Road. Said he'd just been released from prison – with a record of child abuse. I was worried, Inspector Lawless. Some of the time I'm in charge of the playgroup. Bob was worried as well. Said I ought to keep an eye open for this Grayson when I was with the kids. By telling me, Bob was just doing what any caring person would."

"And what did you do with this information?"

"What I just told you. Kept an eye open." Maureen paused and then added, "I tell a lie. I checked with Bob that the school knew all about him as well. That's all."

"And what about you?" Clare said to Carl Greenacre.

For once he wiped the jolly expression from his silly face. "I didn't think Poplar Road was a good idea for a man like him – it's a stone's throw from the infant and junior school – but what could I do about it?"

"As you know, someone did do something about

it," Brett snapped, butting in impetuously. "And you were surprised when we asked if you knew anyone with the initials RW. That's because you knew it was Tom Grayson."

"I had no idea who you'd found dead," Carl returned. "If I was surprised, it was because you were asking about *any* initials. I didn't know what it was about. That's all."

Giving a false smile because she didn't believe the Greenacres, Clare asked, "Who else did you tell about Grayson?"

Assuming his role as leader again, Carl took it upon himself to answer. "No one. But…" He paused theatrically.

"What?"

"Well, I don't like to say this – don't like to get anyone into trouble – but I remember Jamie Lennox was on the next table in the café. I caught his eye at one point and reckoned he was listening in on what we were saying."

"I see. Mr Lennox again."

The Greenacres nodded in unison.

"Thanks," Clare said. She and Brett got up. "That's all for now," she said. With undisguised menace, she uttered, "But I'm sure we'll be back."

Outside in the refreshing mist, she murmured to her partner, "The Greenacres don't like to get anyone into trouble but they seem to make an exception for Lennox. They've provided another dagger to thrust into him."

"Another fictional one?" Brett queried.

"I reckon so," Clare judged. "I'd have thought even you would pick up the body language. They even invented a chat in the café, rather than in the pub, to allow a teetotaller like Lennox to get in on the conversation. Don't you think Carl was telling great big fibs?"

"But my opinion – or yours – doesn't count for anything in court."

"So, let's go back and get whatever we can out of Chelsea's mum," Clare said. "Let's see if she condemns her boyfriend."

Before they marched into an interview with Laura Magnall, hoping that they would be able to wring the answer from her and bring the mystery to an end, Clare and Brett called in at the incident room to see Liz. "Yes," she told them, "all done. I work fast. One day, exactly a week before Grayson saved a lot on gloves and footwear…"

Clare groaned, "That's awful, Liz!"

"In this job," she retorted, "you've got to laugh or you'd cry all the time. Anyway, do you want to know how brilliant I've been or not?"

"Yes, we do," Brett said.

Clearly, Liz was feeling good. Her evening must have worked out well. "A week before Grayson popped his clogs, one of the Greenacres made lots of calls to just about everyone who lives in Poplar Road and Poplar Close – apart from Tom Grayson, of course. Almost as if they were arranging a meeting of the neighbourhood."

"Interesting," Clare replied.

19

A distraught Laura Magnall had been waiting, sitting on an unforgiving chair in the awful blankness of Interview Room 2, for about three-quarters of an hour before Clare and Brett turned up.

"I'm not … used to all this. Horrid place!" The harassed mother shook her head.

"Just a minute,' Clare said, taking a seat. "We've got to record this interview. First, there's some formalities." Once again, Clare found herself introducing the session. "Thursday 7th August, ten-forty in the morning. Interview with Laura Magnall. Officers present: DI Lawless, DS Tilley and…" She turned questioningly to the officer who had been standing at the door while Laura waited.

For the sake of the recording, the constable shouted out his name.

"Right," said Clare.

Brett settled back in his chair, intending to watch his partner drag Laura to the end of her tether.

"As you know," Clare began, "we're investigating the death of Tom Grayson in Oughtibridge. We have some concerns about the role of a number of people in this death, including your daughter, Chelsea. Before we interview her, we thought we'd give you an opportunity to tell us what you know about this incident."

Looking helpless, Laura muttered, "What do you expect me to say?"

"You stated that Grayson had been killed in the burnt-out cottage and his body taken to the reservoir. Is that right?"

She nodded.

"Can you say it in words?" Clare requested. She waved towards the recorder. "For the tape."

"Sorry," Laura said. "Yes. I heard that's what happened."

"How was he killed? Did you hear that?"

"I don't know," she croaked. She shuffled uncomfortably.

"Who told you what happened? Chelsea?"

"No."

Clare persisted. "Who then?"

"Just general chit-chat in the village, I suppose."

"Do you know anything about Tom Grayson?"

"I don't think so," Laura answered cagily.

Clare enquired, "How well – or badly – does Jamie

get on with the Greenacres?"

Suddenly, Laura's stress levels made a quantum leap. "Jamie?" she gasped.

Exploiting her sensitivity straightaway, Clare stated in a cold, matter-of-fact tone, "We're looking into your boyfriend, Jamie Lennox, as well. Actually, we've got a good deal of evidence against him, including shoe impressions near the cottage and Grayson's blood in his boat – used by Jamie and Chelsea sometimes."

Laura became alarmed. "Anyone could use his boat," she claimed. "Not just Jamie or Chelsea."

"And could anyone use his shoes?" Clare retorted.

Laura did not have a response.

"I repeat," Clare said, "how does Jamie get on with the Greenacres and Pillingers?"

Unwillingly, Laura admitted, "He doesn't. Not really. He's not into the drinking thing."

"Does he ever go to the Oughtibridge café?" Brett put in.

"Not that I know of."

"So why do you think Jeff Pillinger and Carl Greenacre provided some evidence against Jamie and a fake alibi for Chelsea?" asked Clare.

"They did what?" she exclaimed.

"After you visited them yesterday, we had a chat with them as well."

Laura was bewildered. "Evidence against Jamie?"

"We rather gathered that they were protecting your daughter and blaming your boyfriend. I guess if they didn't get on well with him, they might do that."

"But…" She couldn't finish whatever she was going to say.

Clare and Brett kept quiet and watched Laura sob.

Eventually she looked up and mumbled, "You said Chelsea's alibi was fake. Maybe what they said about Jamie was fake as well."

Clare leaned forward. "Now, why would that be?"

"Like you said. Because they don't get on."

"Isn't it a bit extreme, though?" Clare proposed. "A bit of a tiff so they accuse someone of murder?"

"Jamie didn't do it," Laura insisted.

"So you're saying they're trying to make him a scapegoat?"

Laura nodded and then, remembering the recording, muttered, "I suppose so."

"Why would they do that?" When Laura looked away and refused to answer, Clare suggested, "Is it because they wanted us to pin it on Jamie so we wouldn't speak to you and Chelsea?"

"Maybe," Laura mumbled.

"So, what do *you* know that they don't want *us* to know?" Again, Clare sat back in a posture that told Laura that she would wait all day for an answer if necessary.

Laura sniffed and shook her head. She peered round the drab windowless room to avoid looking at the two detectives.

"We've easily got enough to charge Lennox," Clare stated, turning up the heat. "And enough to give your Chelsea a good grilling." Clare spread out her arms lazily and said, "You might be able to spare them both that."

Laura's lips tightened into a thin line as if she was trying to resist blurting out her story. But her eyes gave her away. They were moist. Suddenly she blinked and a large tear trickled down her left cheek, leaving a shiny track. Her mouth opened as if gasping for air. "It's not Chelsea or Jamie! It's nothing to do with them. It was me!"

"You?" Clare stared at the woman sitting opposite her and then briefly at Brett. Her partner was looking as surprised as Clare felt.

"Carl told me all about Grayson," she admitted. "He lived just along from me – near Chelsea! And Debs. Lots of boys and girls. And there's the school. Who knows what he might…"

Softly Clare asked, "What did you do, Laura?"

She wiped her nose and mouth, on the verge of disintegrating completely. "I had the neighbourhood to think of. I killed him!"

"How?"

"I … I hanged him."

Clare sighed with both relief and disappointment. Laura Magnall's knowledge condemned her.

Brett was looking even more perplexed than before. "On your own?" His question was almost an exclamation of disbelief.

Laura was a slender forty-year-old woman. She must have been several centimetres shorter than her victim and weighed considerably less. She did not appear to have the physical strength to abduct a man like Tom Grayson, lift him on to some object at least a metre off the ground, tie a cord around his neck and hang him.

"Yes," she whimpered.

"What did you put him on to get the height, Laura?" Brett enquired. His tone was kind but still disbelieving.

"It was … a small stepladder," she replied.

"Where is it now?" asked Brett.

"It's … er … I don't know."

"How did you lift him up on to it?" Clare queried. "I don't think *I* could've done it on my own. Must have been a struggle."

"Well, I did it," she sniffed.

"Come off it, Laura!" Brett said. "Was he conscious? Didn't he fight back?"

All of a sudden, Laura realized that her account was not credible. She looked startled and panic-stricken.

"Who are you shielding, Laura?" Clare asked. "Chelsea and Jamie?" Already Clare was convinced that she knew who was responsible for Tom Grayson's cruel punishment but she could not put words into Laura's mouth. She would jeopardize the value of Laura Magnall's testimony if she became too suggestive. She had to force an answer by reminding Laura that her daughter and boyfriend were still in the firing line. "It sounds to us as if you're trying to protect Chelsea and Jamie with this story."

"No, I'm not!" she cried.

"You see," Clare explained, "we can't understand why you owe anyone anything – except Jamie and Chelsea. So, if you're shielding someone, we reckon it must be them. You wouldn't hesitate to point the finger at someone else because you're not attached to them."

"All right," she wheezed. "I'll … I'll tell you." She didn't bother to wipe away the tears that now flooded down both sides of her haggard face.

In the bland interview room, Laura sobbed, "We had a pact not to tell anyone. I said I wouldn't. And I tried not to, but … if they start telling lies about Jamie…"

"Who's 'they'?" Clare asked kindly, attempting to ease the passage to the truth.

"It's…" Laura shrugged, "…just about everyone. The grown-ups anyway. We kept the kids out of it. And Jamie. He wasn't in on it. He tried to talk me out of it. He's the most innocent of everyone. He even tried to stop us."

Judging that it was time to switch tactics, Clare reached across the table, touched Laura's arm and said, "Tell us what happened, Laura. From the beginning."

Laura Magnall was crushed by the weight of

remorse and plagued by the dreadful pictures that she would never banish from her troubled mind. "It was Carl and Maureen," she began. "They heard about this child molester in Poplar Road. It's not right. So near the school and among our kids! We had a meeting in The King's Arms. The Greenacres and all the parents in Poplar Road and the Close. Carl and Jeff said we should get him out of Oughtibridge. Everyone agreed. No one wants his sort. First, the people in the local shops refused to serve him. But he just got the bus into Sheffield. Ignoring him didn't work so some of the men tried to frighten him. You know, notes and stuff through his door, bricks through his windows. Still no reaction. Carl, Maureen, Jeff and Kath went to see him. Told him he wasn't wanted in the town. They warned him but he refused to move out. He said he was sick of being pushed around."

"So someone decided to take more drastic action."

Laura nodded. "Carl and Jeff led it. Got to get rid of him, they said. I agreed. I thought they meant drive him out but…" She wept for at least a minute before she could speak again. "There was a plan. We'd take him that Thursday and rough him up a bit – just till he said he'd go. We thought, if we all show up, he'll see how much we all hate him and his sort. He'll cave in. But he didn't. He said he'd changed. He said he wouldn't harm anyone any more. But we didn't believe him. Then it all got out of hand. No amount of beating was going to shift him. Jeff had this idea we could hang him in the old cottage. Like old-style justice. Hanging, then it was over and done with. We could go back to how it was before. Safe for the kids. Lots of people agreed. I guess their blood was up and they got carried along with the tide. The rest, like me, were persuaded." Laura paused and, almost inaudibly, muttered, "It's hard – useless – to swim against such a strong current."

Staring down at the table top, Laura shook her head. "Carl said we could make it look like suicide. That was the idea. That's what this man – this monster – deserved, everyone said. Jeff put tape over his mouth and round his arms and legs. Stopped him shouting or fighting. Then it was up to the cottage." She stopped and swallowed before carrying on. "They put a couple of people on the door to make sure the youngsters didn't turn up and see what was going on. You know, Josh and his crowd. Maybe even Chelsea and Debs. But no kids came. Jamie did, though. He wanted us to stop. Shouting about us not having the right to hurt him, even if he was a child molester. There was some bickering and a brawl. Jamie didn't stand a chance. He was sent packing." Almost without taking a breath, Laura stammered, "The men were holding him, Grayson, and tying the noose, putting it round his neck. He was terrified – like a trapped animal. The look on his face…" She held her head and groaned. There must have been a hideous unshakeable image in her brain. "He didn't look like a monster to me. He looked … pathetic.

Scared silly. Most of the women were shouting furiously, baying for blood. They were hysterical. Like those films with witches being lynched and killed. It was a kind of medieval rage. As if they'd got hold of the Devil himself. We were determined to get rid of him once and for all."

Clare turned and called to the constable on the door, "Tissues."

He nodded and disappeared out of the door.

"Jeff Pillinger had a stepladder. He got up and fixed the cord to the roof. Round a rafter. Then…" She gulped but it was too late. Some saliva ran down her chin. It leaked from her like the guilt. "They pushed the man up the ladder one step at a time. His eyes were nearly popping out of his head. Petrified. Such a long way up. Then we all went quiet and Carl kicked the ladder away. He came down – horribly. There was this awful noise from his neck. Terrible. I've never heard… He jerked once, unnatural like, and then swung. Back and forth. The only noise was a creaking. The rope or the wooden rafter. It was … ghastly. This … thing swinging, like a heavy sack. Not like a human being at all. That's what we'd done. Turned him from a human to a thing. I didn't know life could just go – just like that. In a couple of seconds."

The constable returned and placed a pile of tissues in front of Laura.

She grabbed one but screwed it up distractedly in her hand instead of using it on her streaming face.

Eventually, she mumbled, "We began to leave. Some – like me – in silence, shocked by what we'd done. A lot on a high." She dropped the first tissue and took another. This time she attempted to mop her eyes, nose and mouth.

"Then what, Laura?" Clare was urging her to finish her story, to explain the amputations and arson. "You'll feel better when you've said it. Get it out of your system."

"We had second thoughts, I suppose. I'm not sure who started it. But someone – it was probably Jeff – said it wouldn't fool a ... path ... patho..." She struggled to find the right word.

"Pathologist," Brett put in.

"Too clever, he said, to miss the signs. You – the police – would know it was murder and come after us. Carl didn't care. He wanted you to find out the poor man was murdered. And he wanted the press to find out. He wanted it across the headlines. Said it'd be a warning to others of Grayson's kind: the moral majority striking back. So Carl wanted us to leave everything alone, just as it was. Confident he wouldn't get caught. But I guess the rest of us got scared." She pressed another tissue to her eyes. "We thought it was enough just to get rid of the man. No more threat to the neighbourhood. We didn't want the headlines. Didn't want you working out it was murder. Just a quiet disappearance. I guess we lost our nerve. We didn't want to get caught. A few others backed Carl, saying we should leave it. He won them over. But most of us wanted to get rid of the body. So someone had to go back and cover up what we'd done. Jeff Pillinger said he'd do it. Said he'd burn the body but he'd need help. We drew lots. Thank God it wasn't me." She sobbed freely again. Obviously, her stomach wasn't as strong as Jeff Pillinger's.

"Who went back with him?" Clare asked.

"Kath Redgrave," she answered.

Brett was nodding slowly as if her disclosure explained something that had been puzzling him.

Laura continued, "The two of them went back to destroy the evidence. I don't know exactly what happened but they said after that his body wouldn't burn away properly!" She wept into a tissue for a while. "They decided to set the whole house on fire and dump the rest of his body in the reservoir, weighting it down so it'd never come up."

"But it did," Clare murmured softly.

Brett interjected, "Do you know how they weighted down the body, Laura? What did they use?"

She shook her head. "I don't know."

"This may sound a strange thing to ask, but did Jamie lay his own drive?"

"What?" Laura stared at Brett vacantly.

"His block paving. Did he do it himself?"

"Er … yes. But…"

"Where did he get the bricks from?"

Still bewildered, Laura answered, "Jeff Pillinger's, I think."

"Laura," Brett said. "I want to ask you something else. Carl Greenacre and Jeff Pillinger tried to pin the killing on Jamie, because he wasn't part of their cosy circle. They were trying to avoid the blame, hoping we'd arrest Jamie and ditch our plans to visit you – in case you shopped them. You're not now making all this up to pin the blame on them, are you?"

"No!" Laura wailed. "Do I look as if I'm making this up? I couldn't make up… It's too horrible."

Brett nodded. "All right. But what about Jamie? The morning after—"

"He was shattered. Couldn't believe what we'd done. I made him swear he'd never tell anyone. He couldn't bring back that man anyway. Now I wish he could. No one deserves…" She sighed so deeply it sounded like a dying woman's last breath. "I suppose he agreed to keep quiet so he didn't get me into trouble. But he was so … tormented, he went to the vicar for … comfort. Didn't tell him everything but I suppose Reverend Hughes guessed what might have happened."

"All right, Laura," Brett said. "I think you've done your bit."

Laura Magnall did not look up. She was devastated by her own revelations. She sobbed, "We wanted to go back to how it was before but we can't, can we? It'll never be the same."

"No," Brett murmured sadly. "And you understand we can't let you go. You've aided and abetted murder. It'll be a very serious charge."

"But you'll let me see Chelsea and then let *her* go?"

"Yes," Brett said. "But not yet. She's best kept here till we wrap this one up. You don't want her back in Oughtibridge till we're done there."

Clare expected Laura to ask what Brett had in mind for her neighbourhood but she was drained and preoccupied. Exhausted, she sank on to the table-top. Clare ended the painful interview.

On the way out, Brett said, "Constable, I think the least we can do is get her a drink. Sort it out, will you?"

"Well, you were right all along, from the first day," Brett said to Clare. "It *was* a gang. Not the type you imagined, though. A gang of adults – lynching a child abuser."

"Doesn't make me feel any better about it. About Laura."

"Nothing to do with Joshua Redgrave's gang. And I guess Deborah Pillinger did get her injury innocently – on a broken window at the cottage. Not a bite by Einstein. But I bet that piece of plasterboard fell out of Jeff Pillinger's van or off his work clothes when he went back to take the body down to the reservoir." Brett paused before saying to Clare, "You always suspected Pillinger was in on it. You expected him to try and frame Lennox."

"I had a hunch," Clare said modestly.

"I'll get Forensics to analyze Pillinger's van for

blood – and his stepladders. And they can check his stock of block paving bricks, *after* we've moved in and arrested him. I don't want to give him advance warning. And I'm going to make myself popular with the Support Group. I want them to sift through every bin bag dumped in the last couple of weeks at the landfill site that serves Oughtibridge."

"Messy. Why?"

"It was something that occurred to me when Laura said Kath was in on the amputations and dumping of the body," Brett explained. "Kath and Jeff must have got covered in blood. Where's the blood-stained clothing? Perhaps they burnt the really soiled items at the cottage. I don't know. But when we went to see Josh on the day after, Einstein was sniffing round Kath Redgrave's bin and she was anxious about it, to say the least. Maybe that was because she didn't want us to see what we might've seen if Einstein had knocked the bin over. Maybe he smelled Tom Grayson's blood in her rubbish – on her trashed clothes."

"Possible. We always reckoned Einstein was our best witness, barking at the Greenacres, now nosing out Kath Redgrave."

"Revenge," Liz announced. "That's what this is all about. Society's revenge."

Thinking about her own attack on her dad's mugger, Clare nodded. "It's a powerful emotion."

"Like the Poplar Close kids beating up a burglar," Brett noted. "Obviously, they go in for home-made justice in Oughtibridge, big time. The parents have handed it down to their kids. They've bred a bunch of avengers."

"Yeah. They cleaned up their community all right," Clare groaned. "With missionary zeal."

"Last night, I checked out records of similar cases," Brett told them. "Quite a few of them. Abusers beaten up and driven away from their homes. I came across one who'd been strangled. And a case of mistaken identity. The chap who was beaten up wasn't an abuser at all. He just looked like the photo in a newspaper article. The most tragic case was the fire-bombing of a place where a child molester lived – but he wasn't home. There was a little girl inside, one of his victims, and she was burnt to death. So much for vigilantes and the people's justice."

With venom, Liz commented, "Usually it's the tabloids who whip up the frenzy."

"This time, I blame the Greenacres, the whole street and mass hysteria," said Brett.

Clare exclaimed, "But you can't arrest the entire neighbourhood."

"I've got news for you," Brett replied. "It's our *duty* to arrest the entire neighbourhood. They've murdered or aided and abetted murder. We've got to grab *everyone* involved if we can."

"Big job," Clare murmured.

Amused at the prospect, Liz chipped in, "Our new custody sergeant'll have to clear the cells, ready for a deluge."

"Names from Laura this afternoon?" Clare queried.

"No need. Liz has got a list from her clever telephone software." Brett looked at his watch. "In five minutes we're up before the Chief. I need to check it with him but I think he'll give us the all-clear – and the support – to arrest the lot. Simultaneous operation, so the first one can't warn the others it's happening."

"A dawn raid," Liz said with glee. "That's the traditional way of doing these things. Catch 'em unawares in bed."

Brett raised a smile. "Yes. You're in on it, Liz. I'll need you to help supervise. Between us we'll tackle the big three. Clare can oversee the Pillingers' arrest, I'll do the Greenacres – it'll be a pleasure – and you can direct the Kath Redgrave operation. OK?"

"You got it. She's as good as nicked."

In the twilight, Clare and Brett watched the cars and vans gathering ominously at the back of the station, ready for the onslaught in the morning. Clare glanced at her partner's frown and realized immediately what was on his mind. He was remembering a similar raid on Upper Needless in their first major case together. That operation had ended with the death of his girlfriend, Zoe. Trying to cheer him up, Clare said gently, "No firearms this time. It'll be OK."

Amazed by her capacity to get inside his head, Brett murmured, "I hope so."

Clare did not expect the same brutality and resistance that they had encountered at Upper Needless. She expected a swift and smooth procedure without casualties. "I'd buy you a drink but

… I'm meeting someone." She checked her watch and said, "Got to go."

Disappointed, Brett replied, "OK. See you at four o'clock." Endeavouring to raise a smile, he added, "Bright and early." Before she was out of earshot, he called, "Mobile phone on all the time till then – in case something happens and we're called to move in during the night."

"Sure," Clare said indifferently. She didn't anticipate any need to amend their plans for storming Poplar Road in the early hours. Until then, she had other things on her mind.

The grass in the park had been refreshed by the recent rainfall. It had regained much of its lush green colour. But in the gloom the man, dressed immaculately in a designer suit and carrying an expensive portable computer, couldn't see the rejuvenated growth. Apparently unaware of the park's notoriety, he strolled across the tree-lined grounds where Clare's father had been assaulted twelve years before. The man was stylish but not imposing because he was short – perhaps five feet six – and thin. Not a prime physical specimen. But his obvious wealth made him distinctive, made him ripe for muggers. In the semi-darkness, he ambled across the grass and between the trees as if he didn't have a care in the world.

In the shadows of the trees, Clare watched him like an angler watches a float for signs of a predator taking the bait. This was her third evening in the park. So far, not even a nibble, but she hoped that it was third time lucky. Despite her promise to Brett, she had her mobile phone switched off, just in case it rang at a vital moment.

Catching sight of a second figure, Clare ducked down, senses alert. He loped across the lawns behind the man with the portable computer. He was hunched forward, with the posture of a chimpanzee, to help him cover the ground quickly without making a sound. In his hand, he carried something large and heavy. He looked like prehistoric man carrying a club, sneaking up on his prey. Clare's eyes narrowed but she didn't move from her hiding place. She merely watched intently.

The smart man did not alter his lazy pace. He didn't hesitate, turn or break into a run. It seemed that he hadn't heard a thing, that he didn't know he was about to be slugged from behind.

Clare didn't enjoy observing without interfering, without helping, but she forced herself to keep out of it. She stopped herself shouting a caution. Surveillance was not her sort of work: it demanded too much detachment. She breathed deeply as the silhouette of the weapon rose above the first man's head. She stood, ready to dash towards the scene of the mugging.

At the last instant the carefree stroller spun round with the grace of an elegant but vicious ballet dancer. Clare winced as the would-be mugger's legs disappeared from under his body. He issued a piercing howl and his baseball bat thudded on to the ground. At the next moment, he hit the ground as well. The man carrying the case pinned him to the damp grass without even having to put down the computer that he was using as bait.

Clare sprinted to him saying, "Neat work. I owe you one."

She knelt down by the assailant and muttered, "Well, well, well. Mr Adrian Telfer. What a pleasure to see you again like this."

Telfer groaned. "My leg. It's broken!"

Clare shook her head and smiled. "I didn't hear anything snap. What you've got there is a dead leg. Believe me, if this gentleman," she nodded towards her friend from the karate club, "had wanted to break your leg, he would have – and you'd know it. You'd deserve it too. But he's too kind."

"I didn't do anything!" he barked, writhing on the ground like a melodramatic footballer after a tough tackle.

"With your prints on the baseball bat? With two witnesses catching you red-handed?" Taking great pleasure in the words, she pronounced, "Adrian Telfer, you're under arrest. You do not have to say anything. But it may harm your defence if you do not mention, when questioned, something which you later rely on in court. Anything you do say may be given in evidence."

*　　*　　*

The city was still asleep when Clare and Brett brought together the team and gave them the final briefing. They'd been through the plan once already on the previous night but Brett recapped and answered any last-minute questions. Big John turned up to hear and approve the arrangements, to check that Brett had completed his paperwork and obtained all of the necessary warrants. And he wished them luck.

A technician wired Brett and Clare then asked for a test conversation. "Can you hear me?" Brett said into the air.

Out in the corridor, Clare adjusted her ear-piece. "Loud and clear."

"Not like last night, then."

"You what?" Clare replied.

"I called you late. Before a big raid, I guess I could've used your company. But your mobile was off and you weren't answering your home phone."

"Sorry, Brett. I was…" She didn't carry on with a feeble excuse. She knew he'd hear sooner or later that she'd made an arrest last night. Instead, she tried bravado and humour, "A woman's got to do what a woman's got to do."

Liz's amused voice cut in. "Testing, testing. Yes, I can hear as well. No more tiffs, please, you two. You're live on air."

"You sound in fine form," Clare said to Liz.

"Because sir's allowing me to go on a school outing," she joked.

Clare chuckled to herself. She guessed that there was more behind Liz's good humour. Sure, Liz was always cheery but there had been an extra sparkle yesterday and this morning. Probably, her new relationship with this chap was blossoming nicely. Clare had not met him but she was pleased for Liz. "It's more than the buzz of an arrest," Clare teased. "When are you seeing him next?"

"Are you after a job as chaperone?"

"That'd be interesting," Clare replied.

"Well, it's tonight at my place and I don't need one. Now keep your telepathy to yourself, Sergeant Tilley."

The technician's voice told them simultaneously that during the operation, they'd be on-line to Control at all times. They wouldn't be wired to each other because they'd suffer information overload: constant white noise crackling in their ears. They could ask for any information direct from Control.

Brett announced, "OK. Let's get this show on the road."

Slowly, the troops filtered out into the dark morning that still felt like night and climbed into the waiting line of vehicles. The weather had not yet made up its mind. The mist might be the prelude to a downpour or it might be dispelled by the sun, when it appeared, providing another blistering day. Clare, Brett and Liz got into the same car and headed north.

They had never had such an easy journey to

Oughtibridge. The roads were almost deserted. There was something peaceful, pure and attractive about Sheffield before dawn. It wasn't just the emptiness of the roads: it was the atmosphere. Traffic had not yet started to blight the streets and belch pollution into the air.

The plan was straightforward. The vans would stop in Church Street and, on foot, the support groups would filter noiselessly into Poplar Road and Close before daybreak. Once each small team was in position outside its assigned house, at exactly four forty-five, three squad cars would barricade Poplar Road. There was only one exit so that precautionary part of the operation would be easy. Brett and a larger team of ten would tackle the more difficult arrest at The King's Arms. The pub was situated on a through road; it was a much larger property than the Poplar Road houses and it had three exits. Brett was careful to make sure that there were no weaknesses in the net that would allow the Greenacres to slip away.

There would be patrol cars stationed on each of the two major and five minor roads that connected Oughtibridge with the rest of the country. Also at four forty-five, when the teams were ready to swoop on the houses, those cars would block the muted roads and isolate the community that had despatched Tom Grayson. The vehicles and officers in them formed an outer barrier ready to mop up any leaks.

Nearing Oughtibridge, Brett asked Clare and Liz, "All right?"

"Yeah," they both replied soberly.

"Let's not have any heroics. Let the big blokes with body armour go in first," Brett said, turning pointedly towards Clare. "We're here to supervise – from the rear. Out of harm's way. We arrest and caution once the support group's got everything under control and secure. I don't want any more injuries for you to complain about, Liz."

"Yes, sir," they both chimed like obedient – and cheeky – pupils.

Clare turned left into Church Street and immediately stepped on the brakes. Behind, the first van of the convoy ran into her back end. The second van shunted the first. Luckily, neither crash was loud or serious, just a couple of bent bumpers and a smashed indicator cover. Neither driver bothered even to get out to survey the damage. There was more important business to take care of.

Unconcerned and unhurt, Einstein strolled out from under Clare's wheels. Clare shook her head and smiled. Accelerating smoothly towards their planned parking spot, Clare whispered, "No sermon, please, Brett. I know I should've run him over to avoid a crunch and drawing attention to ourselves, but—"

"I wasn't going to say a word," Brett told her. "You can't splatter the hero of the piece in the road. Besides, he's my mate."

It wasn't like a normal operation. Usually, a team had one goal: the arrest of a single suspect. And everyone focused on that one aim. It provided a team spirit that sustained everybody. This time, the operation was too large for any one officer to own. It lacked community spirit. As the troops disgorged silently from the vehicles and crept towards their designated houses, they each concentrated on their own target. They didn't want to be the ones to let down the entire team and so each officer cared less about the overall effort and more about their own piece of the action, determined not to fail.

Brett pushed his car door closed rather than slamming it shut and then breathed in the damp air. Einstein raced up the verge and came to an abrupt halt next to him. To get Brett's attention, he threatened to bark loudly. Brett knelt down and patted the dog. "Thought you'd be inside at this time. Didn't bring a treat," he confessed. "But I do need you to be quiet and out of the way. There's a bone in it for you if you're good. I'll speak to Jamie Lennox about it."

Einstein seemed to understand Brett's need. When Brett opened the car door again, the retriever leapt inside and Brett shut him in.

Just before Clare and Liz departed with their own teams, Brett breathed, "Good luck!" He set off down the road towards the pub with his support.

To Liz, Clare said, "Well, you've been hankering after this bit of excitement for some time: crawling along in the dirt below the level of the walls and hedges. I hope you think it's worth it. You can tell me after."

They went their separate ways with black-clad officers.

Four forty-three. There were still forty-seven minutes before true sunrise. Seventeen minutes to the first light of day. Only two minutes to zero hour. Everyone was in place. Silence had returned to Oughtibridge. Clare was poised with the seven members of her support group, out of sight behind the Pillingers' unruly hedge. Despite being the only woman in her crew, she did not look out of place. Her physique matched that of her male colleagues, her poise and athleticism exceeded theirs. She remained calm and confident. She was more concerned about her partner. After the events at Upper Needless, Brett would not be so relaxed. With thirty seconds to go she hoped that he had his mind firmly on the Greenacres. Thoughts of Zoe could intrude at some less critical time. A drop of sweat rolled down the cheek of the officer next to her but Clare remained composed. She could feel the adrenalin in her veins. She needed that. But she could also control it, use it to her benefit. Heightened awareness. Heightened reflexes. Heightened energy.

Eyes on her watch, she counted down, "Five, four three, two, one. Go! Go!"

The Pillingers' front door succumbed to the force of the first two officers. In the close, many doors crashed open but Clare concentrated only on her own job.

Speed was everything. Within seconds of the entry, the occupants of the house could be woken, out of bed, alert and in fighting mood. Clare wanted the Pillingers handcuffed and subdued before they'd had time to rouse themselves. In a well-rehearsed manoeuvre, one officer stayed by the front door, two took the downstairs rooms and back door – just in case – while the others stampeded upstairs at once. Clare was right behind them, taking two steps at a time. Really, she would have preferred to be leading from the front but, as Brett had pointed out, her colleagues were fully kitted for any violent confrontation. It was their responsibility to deal with any resistance. Clare was under strict instructions not to get injured again.

There was no opposition. One officer barred the door to Deborah's room, keeping her out of it, while the others burst into her parents' bedroom. Jeff had leapt out of bed but was not fully awake until two policemen had him by each arm. He was wearing a lurid pair of pyjamas in green and red. Jeff's wife stayed in bed, pulling the sheets up to her chin as if they could prevent her arrest.

Clare stepped forward and announced, "Jeff Pillinger, I'm charging you with the murder of—"

Without waiting to listen to her, Pillinger spat, "If you'd done your jobs properly in the first place and put Grayson away for life, we wouldn't have had to sweep up after you, clearing up the mess you cops left behind! But I'll tell you one thing: you'll never pin it on me."

Clare smiled and pointed to the tiny microphone attached to her shirt. "I already have," she announced. "We've recorded what you just said. Pretty damning, I think." Clare continued the arrest and cautioned him. Then she looked him up and down and, with a grin, added, "You should be grateful I'm not doing you for possession of an offensive pair of pyjamas as well." Before applying handcuffs to his wrists she allowed him the dignity of getting dressed.

Two men escorted Pillinger away, ignoring the shouted insults from his daughter's room.

The male officer remaining with Clare turned his back while Clare watched Mrs Pillinger get out of bed and slip into some clothes. Then, before she was removed from the house and taken into custody, Clare charged her with being an accessory to murder.

Her task complete, Clare perched on the edge of the bed and, for the benefit of Control, said, "Pillingers secure. Any news from Brett?"

The ghostly voice in her ear reported, "Not yet."

"I hope no news is good news. Any problems anywhere?"

"One team's called for paramedics. Suspected heart attack by a target. Old man. Probably mild."

"Can you plug me into Sergeant Payn?" Clare asked.

"Sure."

The commotion from Number 12 was fed directly into Clare's head. The noise was confused, voices superimposed on thunder. Occasionally, Clare made out an utterance from Liz. Clare gathered that Kath Redgrave had been captured but she was objecting vociferously to the presence of men in her bedroom. Liz volunteered to stay with her alone while Kath dressed.

Clare sucked in air. "Dangerous," she muttered to herself. "Don't do it, Liz!"

"Remember," Liz was saying, "they'll be right outside the bedroom door. In like a shot if you try anything funny."

On hearing escalating shrieks from Deborah,

Clare went to tell her what had happened. She informed Debs that a police officer would remain stationed at the house until Social Services arrived. They would have to call at every house where juveniles were left on their own.

All the while, Clare received disembodied mumblings from Number 12 through her miniature speaker. A few exchanges between the two women. Liz calling her support back into the bedroom. Despite Clare's misgivings it all seemed calm and smooth. Then Clare caught Liz's clear and confident voice saying, "Control. We're done here. Coming out now."

Clare breathed a sigh of relief. Another one wrapped up. She wished that she'd had an update on Brett's progress but at least she and Liz had completed their tasks successfully – without complications. She had always expected Brett to take longer. His was the most difficult job. Somehow, in her mind, she saw Carl Greenacre – that sinister clown – springing a nasty surprise, but she had no idea what it could be. There was no basis for her worry – only her concern for a partner who might be distracted by thoughts of a previous raid that had turned into a disaster. Then, as she was about to go down the staircase, Clare heard something in her earpiece. The definite sound of others thumping down the stairs in Number 12. Then a loud cry, "What's going on?" A male voice. Deep but probably young. Clare put her hand to her ear and listened carefully. The voice snarled, "Leave her alone!" The three words became increasingly loud, presumably because whoever had uttered them had closed in on Liz very rapidly. There was a scream, a crash, the unmistakable sound of a fight. Then a different, distressed male voice roaring from a distance. It was one of the support group shouting to make sure Liz's microphone picked up his words. A shudder ran down Clare's spine as she heard the plea, "Paramedics to Number 12! Officer down. We've got a serious situation here. I repeat, officer down!"

Clare jumped up, ran out of the Pillingers' house into the dawn, and sprinted towards Kath Redgrave's home.

Ignoring his own orders, Brett charged into The King's Arms alongside his back-up. As intended, three of the group dispersed to each of the exits. While the rest of the pack rushed to the gate at the end of the bar, Brett took a short cut and vaulted straight over it. On the way, his trailing foot caught one of the pumps and beer splashed out of the tap. Suddenly at the front of the charge, Brett barged through the door marked "Private" and found himself in a long dark corridor. He dashed to the end and hurtled up the plush stairs. The thick carpeting deadened the noise. From the landing, there were several closed doors into the Greenacres' quarters. Brett had no idea which one would lead to their bedroom. He put a forefinger to his lips and directed pairs of officers to different doors. He waved one towards the top of the stairs, to guard the way out. Then he nodded and they spilled into the rooms. One pair stumbled into a bathroom, another found themselves in the Greenacres' private lounge and the others pitched into a spare bedroom. A fourth door opened and Carl Greenacre boomed, "What the hell—?"

The landlord didn't need an answer. He knew. Deserting his wife, he scurried into the last room – their kitchen – and pushed something heavy against the door.

One female and one male officer went into Maureen's bedroom to arrest her. Impatiently, Brett stood outside the kitchen and yelled, "This isn't going to help, Carl. You're stuck in there. Surrounded. You can't escape!"

There was no reply.

Brett stood back and nodded towards the door. Two of his support group began to work on it till it shook with their force. But it didn't give way.

Abruptly, Brett had a chilling thought. Perhaps, in a public building like this, there would be a fire escape from the upstairs quarters. He shouted, "Keep at it!" and dived towards the stairs. "Two follow me!" he commanded as he flew down the steps. He raced along the corridor and back into the lounge. The officer at the main door stood to one side as Brett ordered, "Stay there."

Outside, the first signs of sunlight were trying to

penetrate the haze. Brett sprinted along the gravel path and through the garden with two officers in his wake. He pulled up at the corner of the pub and cursed under his breath. An iron ladder, hanging down from the kitchen window, was attached to the west wall.

Brett surveyed the ground at the back of the pub and said, "Control, Carl Greenacre's on the loose. On foot. Alert all officers in the outer ring."

Then one of his support group cried out, "There!" He was pointing to a path that led over Coumes Brook and into the small wood behind the town. Looking bizarre in his night-clothes, the landlord had turned left and was jogging up the slope in the direction of Onesacre. His indistinct figure scattered the mist.

Brett muttered, "Here we go again!" He broke into a run. It felt good. He had missed his usual morning jog and the chase made up for it, even though he preferred to run for pleasure. To Control, he said, "He's headed towards Wheel Lane. Tell the car we've got up there. But I reckon I'll have him before that." Already over the stream, Brett was leaving his colleagues behind and gaining on Carl Greenacre. He stretched his powerful legs a little more and swerved round a tree. Not yet panting, Brett asked, "How are the others getting on?" He seemed to be talking to the wood.

A squirrel turned tail and bounded up the nearest tree.

"All teams reported in. But…"

"What?"

"Two've called for paramedics. One suspect with a mild heart attack. A police casualty at Number 12."

Brett leapt effortlessly over a fallen trunk. Carl Greenacre was not far ahead, struggling to keep his weary legs moving. The haze was not dense enough to obscure Brett's view of his quarry, only metres in front. And daylight increased with every passing minute. The landlord was having trouble keeping his balance, running on bare feet. Brett could hear Carl's shrieks of pain as his soles slapped down on a sharp stone or a twig.

"Number 12," Brett muttered. "That's—"

"Sergeant Payn's outfit."

Brett's blood ran cold. "Not Liz," he groaned to himself. "Please."

Control heard his private prayer and responded, "No details yet. Could be any of her team. Don't even know the extent of the injury."

Spurred by the bad news, Brett summoned extra energy and lengthened his stride. He didn't want to be on the edge of this wood, chasing a stupid suspect with a ridiculous haircut. He wanted to be at 12 Poplar Road. He accelerated and dived.

Brett tackled Greenacre roughly round the waist. He made no attempt to soften the landlord's fall. He didn't feel like being gentle. He just brought the pursuit to a hasty, untidy end.

Greenacre landed on the ground like a punctured

football. He came to an abrupt halt and air rushed out of his mouth. He lay there, winded, deflated and moaning.

Once the two back-up officers were within sight and closing in, Brett shouted to them, "Book him! I'm off." He turned on to the footpath on his left. It went back into the wood and emerged between houses into Church Street, not far from Poplar Road. Brett raced across the road and up the lane towards the three squad cars that marked the edge of the main operation. Already, suspects were being led away one by one in separate cars so that they could not talk to each other. It looked as if the place was being forcibly evacuated like some war-torn village. Some of the prisoners of war would be driven to Sheffield, some to Barnsley, others to Rotherham. Brett had to use cells in other South Yorkshire police stations because he would have outstripped Sheffield's capacity. Right now, though, he was more concerned with the events at Kath Redgrave's property.

It had all gone beautifully according to plan. Liz
posted one beefy guard outside Joshua Redgrave's
room even though the lad was sleeping soundly
through the raid. Three officers and Liz burst into
Kath's bedroom before she was properly awake.
Kath sat up in bed, swore, and threatened the
intruders before she realized that her unexpected
and unwelcome visitors were police officers coming
to charge her with aiding and abetting murder. Then
she cursed again.

Liz did not handcuff Kath immediately. She
invited her to get dressed.

"What?" Kath exclaimed. "With them looking
on?" She jabbed a finger accusingly at the male
contingent.

"They'll turn their backs," Liz promised.

"They'll do more than that," Kath insisted. "They'll leave my room."

"I shouldn't, but... All right," Liz agreed. "I'll stay and the men'll leave. But remember," she warned Kath, "they'll be right outside the bedroom door. In like a shot if you try anything funny." Disregarding her colleagues' objections about correct procedure, Liz ushered them out of the bedroom.

"Well, at least you're civil about it," Kath muttered.

Liz nodded towards the door that she had left slightly ajar. "I wouldn't want that lot watching me, either." Wary of being too civil with a woman who had taken part in a hanging, grim amputations and the calculated dumping of a body, Liz said sternly, "Hurry up and dress." She extracted some handcuffs, ready to apply them to Kath's wrists.

Stumbling into a pair of jeans, Kath retorted, "All right, all right. I'm not at my best at five in morning, you know."

When Kath was decent, Liz called her support back into the bedroom and locked the suspect's wrists together. Reporting the conclusion of a successful hit, Liz said, "Control. We're done here. Coming out now."

The support group descended the staircase first, followed by Kath Redgrave, and then Liz at the rear.

Above them, a confused Joshua appeared at his bedroom door. He cried, "What's going on?" Seeing a man outside his room and his mother being abducted, he panicked, grabbed a knife from his chest of drawers and thrust it at the officer. The man leapt back immediately to avoid the thrashing blade. Josh slipped through the gap and on to the landing and dashed down the stairs in a rage.

"Leave her alone!" Josh snarled as he rushed to protect his mother in the only way he knew: with a passionate physical attack. He might not even have grasped the fact that the people pounding down the stairs, taking away his mother, were police officers.

The moment seemed to pass in agonizingly slow seconds. Josh was in a dangerous state. Still sleepy, not hearing or comprehending the shouts of "Police officers! Freeze!" Acting on sheer impulse. Frightened for his mum. Quicker on his feet than the man who was guarding him.

Liz was trapped. Below and in front of her there was Kath and a cluster of policemen. Above and behind her there was a furious hysterical Josh. And a knife. There was no room for her to manoeuvre on the staircase. Unlike the officer on the landing, she could not dodge Joshua's despairing thrust. She could not shield herself from the blow to her shoulder and neck. The knife struck above her body armour.

She screamed and fell into Kath Redgrave. Two of the back-up team grabbed Kath and whisked her away. The officer who had been upstairs clutched Joshua and smashed the boy's hand down on the banister, loosening his grip on the knife. It fell with a clatter into the hall below. Another member of the team took one look at Liz sprawled down the stairs, and roared so that her microphone picked up his words, "Paramedics to Number 12! Officer down. We've got a serious situation here. I repeat, officer down!" He yanked off his shirt, revealing the body armour underneath. Screwing up the shirt he pushed it with both hands against the gaping wound in Liz's neck, applying as much pressure as he dared to staunch the alarming flow of blood. Then he looked up at his colleague and nodded towards the small gap between Liz's inert body and the rail. "Get him out of here!"

Josh was suffering from shock, just as dumb-founded as those who had witnessed his panic attack. When the policeman pushed him forward, he went willingly, unable to take his eyes off his handiwork. As they edged past Liz, Josh muttered pathetically, "I didn't mean to... I'm sorry. I didn't know what was going on. I didn't mean to hurt her."

As soon as Clare saw Josh being led away, his bare right arm glistening with deep red splashes, she knew. It was the colour of fresh blood from an artery. She gasped and ran to the front door. Inside, one of the support group was crouching half way up the staircase, trying to close the awful wound in Liz's neck and whispering into her ear, "Hold on! Medics on their way. You can make it."

But Clare looked at the extent of staining on the stairs and realized that Liz had already lost too much blood. Despite the officer's efforts to staunch the dreadful flow, despite his hopeful words, he could do nothing for her. Clare's worst fears about knives had been well-founded. The weapon that had haunted her ever since Telfer's attack on her father had blighted another life.

She clambered up the stairs, alongside the policeman. Liz had tied back her shiny black hair for the operation but it had come loose in the attack. Now it was splayed untidily over her shoulders and the steps. Some of it was matted grotesquely with blood. Clare said to her friend, "Liz, it's me. Clare." She took her unresponsive hand and squeezed it. "You did fine. I'll tell Brett. We're proud of you."

Liz did not react.

Below, Brett burst into the hall. As soon as he saw Liz, he froze, stunned. A glance into Clare's dismayed eyes told him everything he needed to know. "Oh, no! It can't happen!"

But it had.

The three cars at the end of the road had been shifted to let the ambulance through. The paramedics tended to Liz but there was no longer a need to hurry. They could not revive her. Outside, the last few suspects were being marched away in a steady stream. Instead of a joyful mopping-up operation, the end of the raid was utterly dismal. Any resistance by the suspects was met not with banter but with bad-tempered force. When the stretcher bearing Sergeant Payn came out of Number 12, the remaining members of the team stopped whatever they were doing and remained silent with bowed heads. The officer who had tried in vain to save her was sitting in the Redgraves' garden like a lonely and overgrown gnome. When he saw the despondent medics carrying the stretcher, he stood to attention with tears on his cheeks. The dejected crew watched the ambulance weaving its way sedately out of Poplar Road. They wished that it had roared away at speed, sirens blaring. That would have meant there was hope. Instead, it went slowly and carefully, respecting its unknowing passenger. Only when the ambulance disappeared into Church Street did the officers resume their work joylessly.

The success of the operation would continue to be overshadowed by grief and bitterness. Even after several of the neighbours had confessed, after Debs admitted that her dad had sent her to the cottage to retrieve a hacksaw in case it incriminated him, and after Grayson's blood had been detected in Jeff Pillinger's van and on clothes reclaimed from Kath Redgrave's and Pillinger's rubbish, there would be no celebrations.

"Brett," Clare said softly to her partner. But she could tell by his distracted appearance that he was listening to a question spoken directly into his ear.

"Two suspects missed, then," he said tersely into

thin air. "Both night-shift workers. Send in back-up. You hardly need me to tell you that. Get them at work." He sounded impatient and upset, as if he should be tending to something else.

Clare put her hand on his arm. "You're busy. I'll call the Chief and tell him."

"Sure?" Brett said to her, ignoring for a moment the unending whispers and annoying enquiries in his head. "It won't be … easy."

She nodded sombrely.

Clare said, "You finish off. I'll tell John."

Brett nodded. "Thanks." He turned his attention back to the unseen Control and snapped, "I missed all that. Say it again. I *have* got … a lot going on down here, you know."

Clare retreated to the quiet of their car and let Einstein out. He sauntered away, apparently disappointed that he'd been dismissed without the promised bone. Or perhaps he detected the pervading melancholy and was also affected by it. Clare plonked herself down in the deserted car, sighed and shook her head. Marshalling as much resolve as she could find within herself, she asked to be put through to Detective Superintendent John Macfarlane.

Before she could issue the painful words, John said, "I hear you got nearly all of them. I dare say Brett'll clear up the last two pretty quickly. Well done. Seriously good work – again."

"Yes," Clare mumbled. "But…" She swallowed and winced. "We lost Liz, sir."

Having another case solved, John was in a good mood. He did not adjust to Clare's tone straightaway. He expected the usual end-of-case jesting and indulged in it himself. "Lost? That's careless of you. Where's she gone to?"

Clare could hardly control herself while she tried to convey the news without breaking down. She was a police officer, trained to deal with any eventuality, but it wasn't always easy. She stammered, "No, sir. I mean, we've lost her. She's…"

John's unbelieving silence cut her like a sword.

In the solitude of the car, she wept.

From the meagre pile of Liz's personal effects, Clare took her friend's front door key. It felt remarkably cold in her hand. Clare breathed deeply twice to gather strength and then set out for Liz's house. She was taking on one of the worst jobs of her life. She would wait in the sad isolation of Liz's house until her new boyfriend turned up, then she would tell him that one of the nicest people in South Yorkshire police had be killed in the line of duty. She would tell him that it was a brave, tragic, pointless death at the hands of a scared boy who was protecting his mother in the only way he'd learned. Clare would offer useless consolation and take a note of his name and address. That way, she could let him know the funeral arrangements. Then, she would tell him that he had to put Liz out of his mind and out of his plans for the future. After that, she would go and see Liz's relatives.

At a red traffic light, Clare wiped another tear from her eye.

John Macfarlane shook his head in despair when he saw the tabloid press coverage. *Cops arrest residents for lynching child abuse fiend. The people's justice on neighbourhood pervert. Community blamed for punishing evil beast.* The articles came close to condoning murder as a just retribution or as a means of protecting children. When Clare Tilley knocked on the Chief's door and came into his office, he swept aside the pile of newspapers before she caught sight of the headlines. She had enough to worry about without knowing that she had been slated in some sections of the press for doing her job. For doing a very good job. Before John could commend her, he too had to admonish her.

Clare did not sit down and John did not invite her to do so. She stood formally to attention in front of his desk, waiting for the reprimand.

"I've got Greg's case notes on Adrian Telfer here. With a postscript. Something about an ... unwanted intervention by Sergeant Tilley. And there's a reference to something similar on the Baird tape – though Brett shut him up pretty quickly. Now, you take time out of a murder investigation to do some unauthorized part-time work to bring Telfer in for attempted robbery. There won't be private investigations on my patch, Sergeant Tilley."

"No, sir," Clare replied.

Big John shook his head. "Some would say you're as bad as Bob Baird. You both acted on personal vendettas. There's absolutely no place for them in this outfit, right? Cheating and entrapment aren't the way to nail the bad guys. I have to say, in the light of these events, the Promotions Panel won't be meeting – not for some time. And, as I've told Sergeant Lenton, we don't like sneaks telling tales either."

"No, sir," she repeated stiffly. A while ago her chances of promotion were very important to her. Now, they seemed trivial.

Big John sat back and exhaled. He seemed tired and drawn. "In the circumstances, all this seems…" He waved his hand vaguely in the air. "I'm sorry about Liz, Clare. We all are. It hurts us all when one of us… Especially one as … valued as Liz."

Clare did not interrupt John's sincere words but she was not convinced that everyone in the squad had always valued Liz. Clare doubted that Big John, as a traditional white male detective, would really understand. She remembered the sickening abuse that Liz used to suffer and the lingering prejudice against a black woman in the force. Clare hoped that those responsible would be thoroughly ashamed of themselves now.

The chief was still trying to find the silver lining around the oppressively dark cloud. "None of us would be here, in this crazy business, if we didn't accept the risk, if we didn't think it was worth it. I'm sure Liz was the same. Like it or not, we have to get used to taking the rough with the smooth. And, as far as I can see, there's no blame to be attached to any of my officers. Certainly not you. Certainly not Brett. Not even me – though I assigned her to the case in the first place. It's one of those things that happens from time to time in the police force."

"You'd better say that to Brett, sir. He's feeling it. He told her to take on the job in the field."

John nodded. "And did he have to twist her arm?"

"She'd been volunteering for ages. If anything, she twisted *his* arm. And I encouraged it as well. She'd done field work before and it seemed like a simple job."

"Then Brett's got nothing to feel guilty about. And we both know Brett's one of the toughest in the squad. He'll pull through."

"I know," Clare said. "And he's probably trying to convince himself of that as well. But I'm sure he'd welcome hearing it direct from you."

"He was going to – when I saw him next. But, on your advice, I'll see him now. Go and get him. It's not all bad news. We may not be in the mood for it but I've got to give you both some good news as well."

After Big John had absolved Brett of any responsibility for Liz's death, he poured praise on Clare and Brett for their work in closing the Grayson case. "You two have got a hundred per cent record for clearing up major crimes so far. I want to tell you I'm impressed." He glanced at Clare and added, "When you stick to the job in hand."

Together, Clare and Brett muttered, "Thanks."

Abruptly and unexpectedly, John announced, "After … what's happened, you both deserve a holiday. I know just the place."

"Oh, yes?" Brett murmured suspiciously.

Perhaps thinking that the best remedy for their misery was distraction, he said, "The Caribbean's very nice at this time of year. At any time of the year. Palm trees and beaches. Very laid back. Tobago. Just the place for a bit of relaxation and recuperation. All expenses paid. And while you're there, the locals have requested our help with a spot of bother…"

Have you read?

LAWLESS & TILLEY

Still Life

MALCOLM ROSE

SCHOLASTIC

1

Kerry picked up a stick and pretended to throw it. Really, she didn't let go and instead hid it behind her back. Copper wasn't fooled. She always did that. He waited, gazing into her face, his tongue hanging out. "All right," Kerry said to him. "This time." She drew back her right arm and threw the stick as far as she could. Copper turned and bounded after it happily.

Copper was an eight-year-old Irish setter – a year older than Kerry. Kerry's dad would often joke, "We got a dog instead of you – because we couldn't afford a baby – but then you came along anyway!" Kerry had grown up with Copper. She loved him and thought of him as *her* dog. She always felt safe in the wood with him. Copper would never let her come to any harm. He was big and faithful and reddish-brown. "The colour of copper," her dad told her, explaining the dog's name. Her father was a chemist, so he should know. As she walked, Kerry twirled the dog's lead in her left hand.

Copper loped back to her with the trophy in his mouth. Dropping the slobbery stick at her feet was his way of dropping a hint. Eagerly, he gazed up into her face. Kerry picked it up by the dry end and threw it again, this time in the opposite direction. Copper galloped after it.

It was the early evening of a sizzling July day. The sun had lost none of its power, so it seemed much earlier than six o'clock. Kerry was feeling good because it was the first Monday of the summer break. No school for the next six weeks. She would be able to walk Copper through the wood at any time every day. Heaven. So much better than a stuffy classroom. She bent down and hugged Copper when he next delivered the stick, but Copper squirmed out of her arms. He was too keen on running and fetching to enjoy an embrace just now. Kerry laughed at him. "Oh, all right." She threw his beloved stick again.

This time, when Copper found it, he didn't grip it between his teeth and charge back to Kerry with it. He was taken with a nearby smell.

"Copper! Here, boy," Kerry called.

The dog didn't respond. He continued the investigation with his nose.

Kerry left the path and headed for Copper, muttering, "What have you found? Daft dog."

At school, Kerry was bright and popular. She was

good at games and was always willing to help anyone in her class with their work, so she had plenty of friends. Even when she wanted to get on with her own schoolwork, she'd stop to try and sort out someone else's problem if she was asked. And she never let on to the teacher if classmates claimed that they had done the work on their own. Kerry's best friend was Farida and their teacher would say, "You two make a good pair. You'll do really well – if you keep your minds on your work and off the nattering."

Kerry's hair was fair, almost blonde like her mother's – the exact opposite of Farida's flowing black hair. As Kerry walked towards Copper, her hair brushed against her shoulders. "Come on, Copper. Let's get going. Where's your stick?"

The stick had been forgotten. Copper was engrossed in something else. His nose seemed to be glued to it.

Kerry leaned on his back and looked down at his find. "What's –?" Then she cried, "Ugh!" and backed off, shouting, "Copper! That's disgusting! Come away."

The red setter was too intrigued with his discovery to obey her. He nudged it with his nose but the creature refused to react. Copper was surprised. Instead, he pushed it with his paw. It should have jumped up and run off or put up a fight. It did neither. It was dead. Reluctantly, perhaps disappointed, Copper abandoned his treasure and padded towards Kerry.

"How could you?" Kerry said to him. "I'm not going to let you lick me ever again – not after you've been round a dead rat."

Suddenly, two people jumped out from behind a couple of oaks. Scared and surprised, Kerry cried out. Copper started to bark ferociously.

With one hand over her heart and the other on her dog's back, Kerry murmured, "It's all right, Copper." To the two boys who had appeared and were giggling at the drastic effect that their prank had caused, she said, "Liam! Makbool! You're pests!" Makbool was Farida's older brother and Liam was his next-door neighbour. They were always messing around and getting into trouble at school.

Liam asked eagerly, "Did you say there's a dead rat? Where?"

Kerry made a tutting noise but waved her hand towards it anyway. "Over there."

"Great! Let's take a look," Liam said.

As they wandered towards it, Makbool said to his friend, "I bet it's all stiff."

"Perhaps it's got maggots," Liam put in enthusiastically.

Kerry left them to it, mumbling under her breath, "Boys!" When she started to walk again, she was tugged back. Her T-shirt had caught on a bramble. She released herself from its grip but only after pricking her finger and sacrificing a white thread of cotton to the barbed shrub. Once she had freed herself, she picked up another stick for Copper and resumed the game as she strolled through the wood.

At the edge of Hallam Golf Course, Copper dropped his stick. At the point where the dry-stone wall was low enough for him to see over, his keen eyes picked out something much tastier. He jumped over the stones and made for the small white ball that rolled towards one of the greens. Simultaneously, two people shouted. Kerry's familiar voice ordered, "No, Copper! Leave it. Come here." A man in outlandish checked trousers yelled threateningly and, angrily brandishing a club, hurtled towards the dog. Faced with such fierce opposition, Copper gave up chasing the ball, jumped back over the wall and returned to Kerry.

The path at the perimeter of the golf course held a hundred fascinating smells. Kerry did not notice but Copper's sensitive nose caught them all and his unending curiosity compelled him to investigate each one. Frequently, Kerry called, "Oh, come on, Copper." She made her way cautiously down the steep path on to the rough track that would take her to the road. Approaching the end of the track, Kerry put Copper back on his lead.

On the pavement beside the quiet road, she saw an old man stumble over a crooked slab and fall to the ground, the shopping in his bag scattering all over the place.

Kerry had been taught to be wary of strangers, but she had also been encouraged to be kind and use her head. The majority of people were harmless, ordinary and trustworthy. Kerry could not imagine that this old man, sitting on the pavement and rubbing his elbows, could pose any sort of threat to her. Besides, there was no one else about to help him. There was a car, parked on the dirt track in the wood, but the driver was nowhere to be seen. Strangely, though, the boot lid seemed to be raised slightly as if it was not properly shut. Kerry looped Copper's lead over a fence post and said, "Stay there a minute. Wait, there's a good boy." She squatted by the old man and asked, "Are you all right?"

The old man groaned, "I'm getting too old for this. But if you'll help me up, my dear, I'll be fine."

Kerry took one of his arms and pulled as he clambered to his feet.

Once upright, he groaned again and glanced back accusingly at the paving stone. "It's a disgrace! I'd write to the council and complain but with my hands…" In explanation, he held out a bony, shaky hand, probably incapable of writing legibly. "Oh well, that's life, I suppose."

Kerry was not sure how to offer sympathy, so instead, she picked up his bag and began to collect his goods, which were littering the pavement. Concerned about her absence, Copper barked. Kerry called in return, "Won't be long."

Peering into the wood, the man said, "Your dog? You won't let him off, will you? He sounds ferocious."

Kerry stood up with a packet of biscuits, almost

certainly reduced to crumbs, and replied, "Oh, he's not. He protects me but he's not nasty." She placed the packet in the bag and looked around for any more spilled items. The old man had lost interest. He let Kerry get on with the job of gathering together his shopping. At the kerb, a big black beetle was investigating his tube of toothpaste. Kerry didn't like creepy-crawlies. She shivered, hesitated and then quickly snatched the toothpaste away from the bug. When she couldn't see any more scattered purchases, she went up to the pensioner and held out his bag.

Still feeling sore, the old man took it from her and said, "Thank you, my dear. That's your good deed for the day done. I wish there were more like you."

Kerry smiled and asked, "Will you be OK now?"

He nodded, with a pained expression on his face. Perhaps he was hinting that Kerry should carry his shopping home for him, but he said, "I think so. I'll be getting on. You'd better get back to that dog of yours."

"All right," Kerry replied, and headed for the track where Copper was waiting anxiously.

The dog's eyes brightened and he wagged his tail enthusiastically when Kerry returned. As she got within a few metres of Copper, Kerry halted. She heard a car door opening behind her. The apparently empty vehicle that had been parked in the wood was not empty at all. A figure emerged and said, "Kerry, your dad sent me."

This person knew her name but Kerry did not

recognize the mysterious driver. Confused, she asked hesitantly, "Who are you?"

"A friend of your dad." The stranger walked towards Kerry. "I've come to take you—"

Kerry did not wait for the end of the sentence. She was too suspicious. She turned her back and made for Copper. But she wasn't quick enough. She felt a strong arm around her body and a hand clamped over her mouth. Her cry was stifled and she was bundled towards the boot.

Aware that all was not well with Kerry, Copper snarled and lunged at her captor. Still attached to the fence post, however, Copper was stopped by his lead. He let out a bark.

Too shocked at first to put up much of a fight, Kerry was dumped into the boot. When she started to thrash about with her hands, they were gripped tightly and bound with cord. Her legs were too confined in the cramped space to kick out. She cried, "No! Help!" Almost immediately, foul tape was slapped across her mouth and any further yells were reduced to useless grunts.

Copper grew frantic. With all his strength, he yanked against the post that restrained him while the driver slammed down the lid of the boot and moved towards the car door. Copper tugged and the post began to give way, churning up the ground at its base. Under pressure, it leaned more and more. After one final, desperate lunge, Copper's lead slipped off the post and the furious dog dashed round the car towards the stranger who had taken Kerry. Before the door closed, Copper's jaws clamped tightly round the bottom of the driver's lightweight jacket. His back legs locked and he pulled tenaciously, as if he were playing tug-of-war with Kerry's father and a rubber ring. He never lost that game. He pulled with a determined growl in his throat. The person in the car grabbed the jacket and tried to jerk it away from the red setter. Copper resisted. The driver decided to slam the door shut anyway, knowing it would bang the dog's head.

As the door flew at him, Copper ducked but bravely kept a grip on the coat. There was a ripping noise, the material tore and the door crashed shut. The car snarled into life. As it accelerated on to the road, turned right and sped away, Copper was left with a mouthful of polyester. With a pitiful whine, he watched the car containing Kerry speeding down the road. He disentangled the sizeable piece of grey material from his teeth, dropped it and sniffed around, trying to decide what to do. After a few minutes of exploring Kerry's lingering smell where the car had been parked, he made for home.